Other Books by Elmer Kelton

Barbed Wire
Shadow of a Star
Buffalo Wagons
Bitter Trail
Hot Iron
Texas Rifles
Donovan
The Pumpkin Rollers
Cloudy in the West
The Smiling Country
The Buckskin Line
The Good Old Boys
The Time It Never Rained
The Day the Cowboys Quit
Captain's Rangers
Massacre at Goliad
Badger Boy
Dark Thicket
Stand Proud
Eyes of the Hawk
Hanging Judge
Joe Pepper
Way of the Coyote
Long Way to Texas
After the Bugles
Bowie's Mine
Ranger's Trail
Texas Vendetta
Jericho's Road
Lone Star Rising: The Texas Rangers Trilogy

Praise for Elmer Kelton

"Elmer Kelton does not write Westerns. He writes fine novels set in the West—like *The Pumpkin Rollers*. Here a reader meets flesh-and-blood people of an earlier time, in a story that will grab and hold you from the first to the last page."

—Dee Brown, author of
the *New York Times* bestseller
Bury My Heart at Wounded Knee

"A marvelous romantic Western that will hold a reader's attention to the very end. Kelton is a wonderful storyteller who has won six Spur Awards. This book must surely climb to the top of his award-winning list."

—*Oklahoman* (Oklahoma City, Oklahoma)
on *The Pumpkin Rollers*

"A big, brawling saga with enough action, character, suspense, history, rage, passion, and wisdom to please anybody who likes their bestsellers bold and relentless. This is his finest."

—Ed Gorman, author of *Dark Trail*
on *The Pumpkin Rollers*

"Elmer Kelton, winner of six Spur Awards, has done it again with his latest novel...a vivid and accurate depiction of how the West came of age during the exciting times of our nation's expanse."

—*American Cowboy* on *The Pumpkin Rollers*

"A wonderfully humorous book with just enough evil in a few of the characters to keep realism alive and well. All this, and the most delightful narrator since Huck Finn."

—*Amarillo News-Globe* on *Cloudy in the West*

"The fast-moving *Cloudy in the West* succeeds as a young adult novel, traditional Western, and an all-around good read."

—*Fort Worth Star-Telegram*

"Kelton is a genuine craftsman with an ear for dialogue and, more importantly, an understanding of the human heart."

—*Booklist*

A TOM DOHERTY ASSOCIATES BOOK
NEW YORK

TEXAS RIFLES

Cover art by Benjamin Wu

A Forge Book
Published by Tom Doherty Associates, LLC
175 Fifth Avenue
New York, NY 10010

Forge® is a registered trademark of Tom Doherty Associates, LLC.

ISBN 0-812-55121-4
EAN 978-0-812-55121-1

First Forge edition: January 1998

Printed in the United States of America

0 9 8 7

One

CLOUD ALMOST RODE UPON THE INDIANS' GRAZING horse herd before he realized it.

The summer sun had been bearing down upon him for hours now, sapping his energy, stealing from him the vigilance that he normally never lost while riding across these fringes of Comanche country. In this unrelenting heat it was easy to drowse in the saddle, to let one's mind roam the thousand miles and more to the smoky battlefields of Virginia.

There, even now, angry cannons thundered and men died in the blast of shellfire.

But here, in these rolling hills that marked the western edge of the Texas cross timbers, it was still and quiet . . . so very quiet.

He saw the horses and yanked hard on the hair reins, pulling his sorrel back into the green cover of post-oak brush. Suddenly wide awake, he whipped his rifle out of its beaded deerskin scabbard. He stepped down quickly to the summer-dried grass and held his hand on the sorrel's nose to keep it from nickering. Cloud's heart hammered, his breath came short.

Gradually he eased and got his lost breath back. Those Indians must have been as heat-sleepy as he was. They hadn't seen him.

That was just a shade too close to heaven! he thought.

He was a medium-tall man, crowding thirty. He was broad of shoulder, strong of back. Three days' growth of beard was beginning to blacken a face already browned by sun and wind. His large hands were leather-tough, for they had known the plow. Yet his legs showed a trace of a bow, too, because he had ridden a horse ever since he had been old enough to lace his fingers into a mane and hang on. He wore a sweat-streaked cotton shirt, buttoned at the loose-fitting collar to keep the sun from baking his breastbone. He carried a Colt revolver high on his right hip and a seven-pound bowie knife on his left, encased in a scabbard made from the hide of a buffalo's tail, the bushy black switch still hanging as a tassel.

Through the screen of brush, Cloud studied the loose-held horse herd and the Indians who slacked in the shade of scattered trees around it. Comanches, mostly squaws. He could see only one man, on the near edge of the herd. The warrior slouched on a bay horse that showed the marks of a collar and a white man's brand on the hip. He hadn't spotted Cloud because he was giving his attention to a slender young squaw who sat as close to him as her black-maned dun would get. The warrior was laughing and talking with the woman while he rolled a fresh-made arrow shaft between his teeth, taking the sap out of it.

These were horses a stray band of Comanche raiders had been picking up in the Texas settlements, Cloud reasoned. Now the wily thieves were working their way north to the safety of those trackless stretches of open grass on the Staked Plains, where they would lose themselves like a whirlwind that suddenly lifts and disappears into air, in a solitude so vast that white men drew back in dread.

Counting in fives with tiny moves of his big hand, Cloud estimated that there were eighty or ninety horses. Many a farmer and cowman had been left afoot to walk and curse. More than likely, a few had lost their scalps as well as their horses. To the Comanche warrior stealing down from his stronghold on the high plains, warfare was a game to be played and enjoyed—an end in itself. To steal a *Tejano*'s horses brought material wealth and a considerable measure of honor. To count coup on the hated *Tejano* and bring back his scalp greatly increased the honor and raised the warrior's status in the eyes of the tribe.

Cloud could still see only the one buck, and he wondered where the rest were. He counted six women, young squaws who remained physically able to make the long forays with their men, to do the menial chores and hold the horses and glory in the fighting manhood of their warriors. That there were six women didn't mean there were only six men, however. Many of the bucks never brought women on these trips. They didn't have to, for a Comanche warrior fortunate enough to have a woman with him thought little of lending her to a needful friend.

The other men must be off somewhere trying to gather up more horses, Cloud reasoned. They must feel sure of themselves, leaving only one man with these squaws to watch the ones they already had. Either they had whipped back their pursuit or they considered it too far behind to worry about.

High time to h'ist my tail and get out of here, he thought. *Only, which way had I ought to run? Wrong guess and I'll butt heads with Lord knows how many Comanches.*

He was no stranger to Indian warfare. He'd had his scraps, and a deep scar on one shoulder to show for it. But he saw no sense in riding headlong into a one-sided battle where overwhelming weight of numbers was sure to grind him down.

There was a time to fight and a time to ride away. Without question, this was a time to ride.

He heard the heavy roar of a rifle from somewhere over the next hill, and he jerked involuntarily. The blast was followed by the staccato rattle of smaller guns. The horses lifted their heads, their ears pricking up in the direction of the gunfire. The buck and the squaws turned too, listening. The buck shook his head confidently to the young woman beside him. Telling her, Cloud judged, that it wouldn't take long.

Cloud eased back afoot until he could no longer see the horses, and until he hoped the Indians could not see him. At least now he knew where the rest of the band was. Good chance to get away.

But he was held by the sound of battle. Somebody across yonder was putting up a good fight.

The trouble with being a reasonable man was that reason all the time wanted to argue with a man's emotions. Reason told Cloud to mount up and spur out of there while he could. But emotion made him wonder and worry about whoever the Comanches had bottled up. How much chance did those people have?

Cloud skirted through the post oak, circled the horse herd and made his way up the off side of a hill, the rifle across his lap. Staying within brush cover, he climbed until he could look out across a clearing at the farmhouse below. It was pretty much the usual Texas frontier farmer's log cabin. Actually, it was almost two cabins, its two rooms built under one roof but separated by a narrow, open "dog run." Each room was buttressed by a heavy rock chimney. Man with a family, Cloud figured. And most of them shooting.

Defending fire racketed from three places—from each section of the cabin and from a heavy post-oak corral. The settler must have had a little warning, time enough to get his horses into the corral and shut the gate. To get them, the Indians were first going to have to kill him. Even then, they would be under close fire from the cabin. Heavy smoke rose from the man's position in the corral and drifted slowly away in the hot breeze.

They sometimes said of Texas gunpowder that if the bullet didn't kill the enemy, the smoke would choke him to death.

He's in a good spot long's his powder holds out, Cloud thought. *But there's four or five horses in that corral, and them Comanches can almost taste 'em.*

He tried to rough-count the attacking Indians, but it was hard to spot them all. Some had found good cover in the tall grass. Others lay behind downed trees that the settler hadn't yet put into his fences. Ten or twelve, Cloud judged. A few were firing rifles. Most used bows. He could see the straight, quick flight of arrows, although at the distance he could not hear them strike the cabin or the timber that made up the corral.

He saw an Indian sprint toward the house, then jerk in midstride, pitching headlong to the ground. That angered the others.

They're determined now, he thought. *They'll stay till they've got the job done.*

He might be able to hit one or two of them from here with the long reach of his rifle, but he wasn't likely to change the situation much. They would dispatch a few warriors to take care of him while the rest went on after the people in the cabin. No use in a man selling out that cheap.

He thought then of the horse herd.

There was this about Comanches: they liked to fight, but they didn't care for suicide. If they saw they couldn't win, they usually pulled back. Cowardice was one thing, good judgment was another. Badly as they wanted those few horses in the corral, they probably would leave in a hurry if they thought they were in danger of losing the others they'd already taken, he reasoned. His one rifle wouldn't do a lot of good here, but it could cut a big swath out at that horse herd.

"Just hang on down there, folks," he muttered, backing away carefully. "The dance ain't over yet."

In the saddle again, he circled back the way he had come. Using the brush to hide him, he made his way to the place from which he had first seen the horse herd. He stepped to the ground, taking his stake rope loose from the saddlehorn and working to the end of it, tying it about his waist with a slipknot. The other end was looped around the horse's nose beneath the bridle.

Dropping to one knee, he steadied the rifle against the trunk of a post oak tree and drew a careful bead on the lone buck. He started to squeeze the trigger but hesitated, hating to. The thought of back-shooting sent a cold chill through him. But he knew the Indians didn't fight by rules.

His sorrel chose that moment to stamp flies. The buck turned, bringing up a big old rifle. Cloud felt the man's eyes touch him, and he fired.

The little squaw screamed as the man pitched forward on the horse's neck and slid to the ground. The horses nearest the shot shied into the rest of the band, creating a shock ripple like a stone dropped in water. Cloud drew his six-gun and fired once from where he was, then moved a little, staying in the brush. He aimed over the heads of the squaws on the far side and fired again. Now the horses were on the move away from Cloud. In panic, the squaws began pulling back. Waving their hands excitedly, they screamed at one another and hurried northward. Cloud fired a third time with the pistol.

He knew they thought they had been found by a group of angry *Tejanos*. He sent another shot plowing into the ground near them, to keep them running.

The horses were running now too, in a southerly direction. Cloud stopped to reload the rifle and put fresh charges in the pistol. That done, he coiled the stake rope and stepped onto the sorrel, the rifle slung over the saddlehorn, the pistol in his hand. He spurred in after the horses, firing occasionally, hollering, keeping them on the run.

Ahead lay the heavy post oak timber. Get these horses scattered in there and it would take hours for the Comanches to round them up.

A few of the horses split off to one side. Cloud elected to let them go, lest he allow the others to slow up and fall back into the hands of the Indians. He pulled up a moment to listen. The gunfire over the hill had stopped. Hearing the noise up here, the warriors probably had pulled back from the house and would be on their way here as fast as they could move. Cloud spurred up, yelling and firing the pistol, pushing his horses into a dead run that the Comanches couldn't stop.

He made it. Looking back as he rode into the brush, he saw that the few horses he had lost were slowing down. But the bulk of the horse herd broke into the heavy timber just moments before the Indians bobbed up over the hill. Under cover, Cloud stepped down again with the heavy rifle in his right hand, the stake rope in his left. Again he looped the free end of the rope around his hips. He dropped his reins and trotted to the end of the rope.

Held close by the reins, a horse might shy at the roar of a rifle and jerk away, leaving its owner afoot. But when the shooter stood off at the end of the stake rope, a horse with any training usually took it with comparative calm. Should the horse begin to run and drag him, Cloud could yank the slipknot and free himself. But that was unlikely, for he had taught the sorrel to stand with the nose hitch.

Dropping to one knee and leveling the rifle barrel over a limb, Cloud aimed at the Indian in the lead. He saw the dust puff in front of the man's horse. The Indian jerked the rein so hard that the horse stumbled and almost went down.

Cloud moved twenty or thirty paces and took a long shot with the pistol. He didn't expect to hit anything at the range, but he could raise dust. The Indians hauled up and milled uncertainly. They plainly thought there were several Texans in the brush. He fired again with the pistol and took advantage of the moment to pour a small measure of gunpowder out of his powder horn into his palm. He followed this with a poured-lead bullet and a thin buckskin scrap for a bullet patch. He rammed it down tight, hardly taking his eyes off the Indians.

For a moment it seemed they were going to come on down his way. He leveled the rifle again, drew a careful bead and squeezed. A horse went down, thrashing.

That was enough. One of the Comanches reached down and pulled the unseated Indian up behind him. Then the whole pack put the heels to their mounts and began to run. They picked up the few horses Cloud had lost, but they were giving up the others.

Cloud loaded the rifle again before he moved, and put fresh charges in the pistol. It looked clear now, but a man never could tell. That was likely to be a mighty mad bunch of Comanches. Losing a battle at that house yonder, losing their stolen horses. Now they would have to sneak back into camp like a bunch of squaws.

Cloud coiled the stake rope as he moved toward his horse. He tucked the coils under his belt, where he could yank them out into use if there came a sudden need for the rope again. He eased into the saddle, still watching warily the dip in the hills where he had seen the Comanches disappear. The only thing a man could know for sure about Comanches was that they were likely to do what he didn't expect. Since he didn't expect them to come back, it was a good idea to watch.

Staying in the brush as long as he could, he angled across toward the cabin he had seen. Good chance the Indians—some of them, anyway—were hanging back to see how many Texans were in that timber. An Indian might not be able to read, but he could blamed well count.

Two hundred yards from the cabin the timber had all been cut away. Besides giving the settler material for his house and fences, this also afforded him a clear view of anyone approaching. It cut down the chance of surprise. But the farmer had left some of the tree trunks where they had fallen, and these had given the Indians some protection from rifle fire. Cloud would bet it wouldn't take the man long to drag these up into a pile.

Moving into the clearing, he could feel the rifles trained on him, even though he couldn't see them. Two dogs set up an awful racket. "Hello the house!" Cloud called, keeping his hands up in clear sight and making no quick moves. Nobody answered him at first, but he saw a slight movement at a glassless window. Then a man stepped out from inside the corral.

Cloud's sorrel snorted and shied away from a dead Indian the others had been in too big a hurry to pick up. Cloud stopped twenty paces from the corral. The two men stared at each other. Cloud finally opened the conversation with, "Howdy."

The black-bearded man who stood there was in his late forties—fifty, maybe, for streaks of gray glistened in the sun. He had the broad, strong body of a blacksmith, the homespun clothes of the pioneer. He studied Cloud, the rifle still high and ready in his hands. Distrust lingered in his brown eyes. White renegades were not unheard of in this country. Now and again there was talk of such men riding with the Indians, turning against their own kind. For all this man knew, Cloud could be one.

"Howdy," the man finally said, evidently satisfied with Cloud's looks. "You one of the bunch that was doin' the shootin' across the hill yonder?"

"I *was* the bunch."

Incredulous, the man lowered the rifle and stood with his mouth open. "You mean to tell me you're by yourself?"

"It ain't the way I'd rather've had it," Cloud replied, getting down.

The settler grunted an oath and shook his head. "Luck. Just puredee luck. But give me luck and you can keep your money." He stepped forward, hand outstretched. "Name's Lige Moseley. Elijah, you know, like in the Bible." The man began to grin, the tension leaving him.

Cloud grinned too. "Sam Houston Cloud. I don't reckon the Bible had much to do with my name, though."

"You must be a sure-enough born Texican to be named after old General Sam."

"My folks always thought a heap of the general."

"Then I reckon you live up to your name. He always was a scrappy old booger."

Moseley turned toward the cabin. Cloud dropped his reins over a post and moved along beside him, looking over this ruddy-faced, bewhiskered settler. Steady as a rock, Moseley showed no sign he had ever been scared.

"Indian-fightin' don't seem like it bothers you none," Cloud commented.

"Fit 'em ever since I was a button. Started back in Tennessee, fit 'em all the way west. Reckon I'll fight 'em clean to the Pacific Ocean."

"You mean you expect to keep on movin' west?"

"What other direction is there for a man to go? Got to move now and again, git to a fresh, unspoiled country. Man sits in one place too long, he just naturally goes stale. Are you a movin' man?"

"Have been, kind of. Ever I find me a place that suits me just right, though, I'll probably light and stay there."

They reached the cabin. Moseley spoke through the open window. "Everybody make out all right?"

"All right," came a woman's voice. Moseley moved on to the other side, beyond the dog run. A boy of thirteen or fourteen stepped out with a rifle in his hand.

"How about you boys?" Moseley asked. The boy, whittled from the same oakwood as his father, stared with open curiosity at Cloud. He said, "We done fine." He frowned then. "Now that we got 'em on the run, Pa, don't you think we ought to chase after them and give them a real proper chastisement?"

The old man proudly laid his big hand on the boy's shoulder. "I reckon if they want to fight some more, they'll come back."

To Cloud, Moseley said, "Raise 'em right, they don't panic at the sight of a few Indians. I've taught 'em this is a white man's land. The Lord meant it for crops and cattle, not for painted heathens and the buffalo. The Lord'll see to it that the Christian man comes out all right, long as he keeps his faith."

He motioned with his rifle. "Downed a couple of them out yonder. We better make sure they're dead. Don't want 'em sneakin' up here cuttin' our throats while our backs are turned."

Cloud said, "I saw one of them as I rode up. He was dead."

Moseley grunted. "Other one's over thisaway, then. Want to go with me?"

Pistol in his hand, Cloud walked along beside Moseley, carefully watching the grass.

"Tall grass, it give them redskins a little of an edge on us," Moseley said. "It was hard to see them. I'd've burned all this off, only I been afraid I'd burn the house down too."

They found the Indian lying on his back, his chest still heaving up and down. He had dragged himself partially under the dead foliage of a downed tree, trying to find shade from the blistering sun. His open eyes were glazed. Fresh blood made tiny bubbles on his lips. Cloud could see a gaping hole in the Comanche's belly.

"Done for," he said quietly. It seemed proper to speak quietly in the presence of a dying man, whether he was Comanche or not.

The old frontiersman nodded. "No easy death, either. It'd be God's mercy to go ahead and put him out of his misery."

"I reckon it would," Cloud agreed. "He's yours."

Moseley raised his rifle and held it a moment. There was no sign the Indian was even aware of what was happening. Moseley raked his tongue over dry lips. The old man slowly lowered the rifle.

"I can't do it. How about you takin' care of him for me, Cloud?"

Cloud was silent a moment, his hand cold-sweaty on the grip of the six-shooter. "I can't either. I can shoot at a man when he's shootin' at me. But one like this . . ."

Moseley shook his head. "He can't bother us none, the

shape he's in. So I reckon now it's just between him and the Lord. He ortn't to've been here, that's all.''

The two turned and started back toward the cabin. Moseley said, ''I'll have to set the boys to diggin'. Job like that can't wait very long in this kind of hot weather.''

''There's another one over the hill,'' Cloud said. ''But I expect the Comanches carried him off. They generally do, they get the chance.''

The Moseley boys were out poking around now for Indian souvenirs. They picked up the dying Indian's bow and arrows and the bull-hide shield that lay where the man had fallen. They held it up and looked through the bullet hole in it.

Moseley stared at Cloud with unabashed curiosity. ''Been tryin' to figure you out. Most fellers that's been through here lately has been yellow bellies headin' west, tryin' to git out of havin' to go fight the Yankees. You don't look like that stripe to me.''

''Well,'' said Cloud, ''I'm not on the run.''

''What *are* you doin'?''

''I'm huntin' for Captain Barcroft's company of the Texas Mounted Rifles. I'm supposed to join it.''

''One of them new Ranger outfits, eh? Out to help save the home folks from the Indians while the rest of the boys go whip them Yanks?''

''Not Rangers, exactly. State troops, more like. But you got the job right—patrol the frontier, keep John throwed back.''

''John'' was a frontier nickname for the Indian—any Indian.

Moseley grinned. ''Well, looks to me like you've done started to work. If that Barcroft asks you for any references, just tell him to come and see me.''

The cabin door opened in front of them. A woman stepped back out of the way. ''Go ahead in, Cloud,'' said

Moseley. Moseley's wife stood in the middle of the plain room, staring at him. She was a gaunt, wide-hipped woman in her early forties, shoulders bent by a hard-lived life of work and strain, face dried by sun and wind. But there was a strong set to her jaw, a sturdy determination in her eyes. Moseley might be a strong man, but he would be no stronger than this woman he had married, thought Cloud.

It took this kind of woman to stand beside a man and keep pushing west, to hold ungiving against a harsh daily existence in a raw land, to stand firm in the face of the savage red tide. She wasn't much for looks maybe, but looks didn't count for much in this country.

"How do," she said. "I heered what you told Lige. You really come by yourself, mister?"

"Yes'm." He had his hat in his hands.

"Well, that's really somethin'. Really somethin'."

Cloud heard a knocking and looked around him for the source of it. Mrs. Moseley said, "Like to've forgot about the youngsters. Would you kindly he'p me move this chest, Mister Cloud?"

The three of them scooted a battered oak chest out across the packed-dirt floor. Beneath it appeared a wooden trapdoor. Moseley grasped an iron ring and swung the squeaky door up. "You-all can come out now. One at a time, don't be a-steppin' on one another's fingers."

One by one, children of various sizes began to appear from the depths of the hole. Cloud reached down and helped each one make his way out. The kids were dirt-smeared from rubbing against the sides of the narrow tunnel. Each of them eyed Cloud warily. They weren't used to strangers.

One of the boys, who looked to be about five, complained, "Why don't you let us stay down there, Mama? It's cooler than up here."

"That's just for the needful times. Snoopy redskins see you-all playin' around the escape hole outside, they'd know what it was. It wouldn't do none of you any good then. Git on outside now, and brush that dirt off of you."

Last up was a girl of seventeen or so, carrying a two-year-old boy in her arms. The girl glanced quickly at Cloud with pretty hazel eyes, then handed the baby to her mother. "It was scared," she said. "Had a hard time a-keepin' it from cryin'. I was a-feered them Indians might hear it and find the hole."

Mrs. Moseley took her baby and rocked it in her arms. The harshness in her face faded to a mother's gentleness. "There now," she soothed the child, holding its cheek to hers. "Everything's all right now. Nothin's goin' to hurt our baby, nothin' atall."

With Cloud's help, the girl finished the climb out, watching Cloud timidly. Self-consciously she began to brush the dirt from her clothes.

"Outside, Samantha," Mrs. Moseley said. "We don't want none of that dirt in the house."

Cloud couldn't help wondering how it would ever be noticed, the floor being of dirt anyway. But that was woman's business, and none of his.

Moseley showed Cloud the escape tunnel. "For the kids," he said, "case the Indians ever swamp us. Comes out in a little clump of brush yonder. Gives the kids a chance to git away. We cover it with that big chest, so the Indians'll never even know it's there."

A chill worked up Cloud's back. Anytime Lige Moseley and his wife put the kids down that hole and moved the chest back over the trapdoor, they were committing themselves to fight to the death.

"Just such a tunnel as that one saved my life when I was a button in Tennessee," said Moseley. "Pa and my uncle, they put Mama and us kids into the tunnel and shut the door behind us. Indians killed them and set fire to the cabin, but they never knew about us. It ever comes to that, my kids're goin' to have the same chance."

Cloud looked at the Moseleys and wondered what it all led to. It wasn't just Moseley, for there were others like him, all up and down the western line of the Texas settlements. This was the kind of life Moseley and a great many others had lived since boyhood, treading on the thin edge of disaster. They didn't follow the frontier, they led it. They were the "movin' kind," always on the go, always looking west. Most men who moved west talked of a better life ahead, and Moseley probably talked that way too, when a man sat him down and started him putting his dreams into words. But it wasn't really the better life that motivated Moseley. It was the search itself that gave him his satisfaction.

What would Moseley's kind do when there was no longer a frontier? Cloud wondered. They were a breed apart, a breed for which civilization had little place once it had benefited from their sacrifice.

Moseley looked out the open window at the distant hill. "We sure gave John a whippin'. He won't forget us."

Cloud frowned. "He won't, and that's a fact. They'll remember this place like a thorn in their foot. You watch, some of the young bucks are liable to be back one day, tryin' to even the score up."

"Let 'em," said Moseley. "We'll be rested and ready."

Mrs. Moseley found out Cloud hadn't eaten anything all day but a little bit of broiled bacon and some dry, hard biscuits he carried in the "wallet" slung across the back of his saddle. She said, "Samantha and me, we'll fix you up somethin'. We're a mite short on flour, but you're goin' to have some fresh bread anyhow. We got coffee if you can drink it without sugar. And there's enough venison to finish fillin' you up."

Cloud protested at their cooking up all the flour when there were so many young ones around, but they did it anyway. Almost every time Cloud glanced in the direction of the girl Samantha, he found her covertly watching him. Her shy gaze would quickly cut away.

He felt sorry for her, a little. She was a nice-looking girl. Chances were her mother had looked like this, once. The girl could be pretty, perhaps, if she lived in a settlement where she could have good clothes and shoes and perhaps some bright ribbon for her blonde hair. It was her hair that caught Cloud's eye. Tied at the back of her head, it hung far down below her shoulders. It looked silky and soft, and he found himself wanting to reach out and touch it. If the girl had any vanity, living far out here away from other people, it must have been her hair. Cloud could tell that it had been brushed a lot.

He said to Moseley, "Your kids miss a good many things, not livin' near a settlement."

Moseley shook his head. "They miss learnin' a heap of devilment. Ma, she teaches 'em to read and write, and they get all the schoolin' they need, just a-readin' from the old Bible." Moseley reached up onto a shelf and took down a huge and heavy old family Bible. He set it down on the table in front of Cloud and opened the cover. "Got all the kids' names in here and the dates they was born. Two that died, they're in here, too. We had to bury them where they was—no markers or nothin'. The only thing in God's world to show they was ever born is this here page in the old Bible."

He paused, his mind running back into memory. Then he asked, "Are you an educated man, Cloud?"

Cloud shook his head. "Not much. Never had time for schoolin', or a place to go, either. I can read easy enough;

my mother taught me that. And I know figures."

"That's a-plenty. Too much learnin' is just a handicap to a man out in this country—puts him to yearnin' after things he can't have. Just know how to read, and know enough figures so them settlement sharpers can't skin you out of nothin'. No, sir, my kids don't git the chance to fool around the settlements there. Settlements, they got all kinds of wickedness and sin—things a young girl like Samantha don't need to know nothin' about. Someday there'll be a young man come along—man like I was a long time ago—and he'll marry her. She'll learn what else there is that she ought to know."

He frowned then. "You married, Cloud?"

Cloud fidgeted. "No, sir."

"Promised?"

"No, sir."

Moseley eased again, an obvious thought playing behind his brown eyes. "You ought to have you a woman, you know. Woman's a heap of comfort to a man—helps take the load off of his back."

"Someday, maybe, when I'm settled down. A man's got no business marryin' as long as he's ridin' around over the country chasin' Indians. He needs to be able to provide her a home."

"A town woman, sure. But you take a girl that's been raised up away from the settlements—one that ain't a-goin' to throw a screamin' fit at the sight of a feather—one that don't mind pushin' a plow and choppin' the wood when her man's got to be gone—she'd be a good wife for a man like you, Cloud. A good woman's the makin' of a man."

He paused, watching Cloud for any sign that the message was taking hold. "You know, my girl Samantha's that kind."

"Yep, I expect she is," Cloud said nervously, wishing the subject would change.

Moseley's oldest son, Luke, pushed through the door, rifle in his hand. Cloud noticed that most of the kids had biblical names. "Riders comin', Pa."

Moseley sat up straight, looking at his own rifle in the corner. "Indians?"

"No, sir, whites. Rangers or Minute Men or some such, I think."

Cloud and Moseley walked out the door and stood waiting. There were twenty or twenty-five men in the bunch. They rode tired horses, and the riders' shoulders sagged with weariness. But most of them held rifles or shotguns balanced across their saddles, ready for instant action.

Riding out in front was a dark-skinned man Cloud took to be a Mexican. Almost even with him came a tall, lean, somber-looking rider who quickly caught Cloud's eye. Instinctively he knew this was the leader. His bearing showed it without any questions asked. Cloud remembered what the colonel had told him when he had handed him his orders.

"Aaron Barcroft is the captain. You'll know him when you see him, for there's not another that looks quite like him. He's a tall, nervous whip of a man, with black eyes that bore through you like an auger. You'll think he's the grimmest man you ever saw, and he probably is; he's had some grim things happen to him. He'll drive you till you hate him, but you'll always respect him, for he drives himself harder than any man."

Captain Barcroft rode up to within four or five paces and stopped. He took one long, unhurried glance about the place and seemed to miss nothing.

"I see you've had trouble," he said. "Anybody hurt?"

Moseley said, "Nobody but Indians."

Barcroft said, "We've trailed that band since yesterday.

They had a sizeable bunch of stolen horses with them. Now we find those horses—most of them, anyway—scattered out in that brush. What happened?''

Moseley explained in colorful detail what Cloud had done, adding a little fiction for good measure.

Barcroft's black eyes dwelt heavily on Cloud. Unaccountably, there was annoyance in them. ''Who are you?'' Barcroft demanded.

Cloud told him. He handed Barcroft the letter the colonel had given him. ''I been huntin' you, Captain. I'm supposed to join your company.''

Barcroft didn't take time to read the letter. He shoved it in his pocket. His voice had a sting to it. ''I'm not sure why you're here, Cloud. From what you did, I gather you might be one of those who joins the Rifles looking for glory and adventure. Well, you'll get little glory here. Or maybe you've come to the frontier to get out of going against the Yankees. If you have, you'll find a steel knife and a stone arrowhead can kill you just as dead as a Yankee cannonball. Might even be slower and more painful.

''I'll warn you right now, this is no place for the lame or the lazy. If you go with this outfit, you'll ride sometimes till you're so weary you can't see. Then you'll get off and fight and climb back up to ride some more. You'll go on short rations and tighten your belt and suck on a pebble because you had no water. You won't enjoy it. No one does.''

Angering, Cloud said, ''I've fought Indians before, and I ain't huntin' no glory! What I did here today I did because it looked like the only thing.''

Barcroft said gruffly, ''It might have been better if you hadn't. Those Indians didn't know how close we were. If they'd stayed here a while longer, we would have caught up with them. We could have wiped them out. As it was, you ran them off. They'll be hard to catch now.''

Lige Moseley's face flushed red. He shoved into the exchange. "Sure, you might've caught them. But it might've been a shade late for me and my family. Besides, between us we dropped three of them, and Cloud scattered their horses. What the hell else you want?"

Barcroft eyed him coldly. "I didn't ask you, but now that you've spoken out, I'll tell you something. You're a fool even to be here. You're miles from any kind of help. Your very presence is a temptation to any stray band of braves that passes through."

"It's a free country. I can settle where I want to."

With bitterness Barcroft said, "And endanger that family of yours? No man's got a right to do that. You load up and move back to where it's safer."

Moseley said, "I been stopped a few times, Captain, but I ain't never been pushed back. I don't start now. Not for the Comanches and not for you!"

Moseley's family had stepped out and stood lined up behind him now. Barcroft looked at them. Particularly he looked at Mrs. Moseley and at the little girls. Cloud thought he could see pain in the captain's eyes.

Barcroft shrugged. "I can't force you, Moseley. I would, if I had the right. If you don't move back, you're a fool. Too many men have gone off to war. Too many families have pulled back to safer ground. Don't you know those who stay will be a better target than they've ever been before? You're staying because of pride, and pride can be a good thing in its place. But look at your womenfolks, your kids, and ask yourself which you value the most—your pride or their lives."

Moseley said, "You got a family, Captain?"

Barcroft was slow in answering. His voice dropped a little. "No . . . no family."

"Then how can you tell me what's best for mine?"

Barcroft said, "I know, Moseley. Believe me, I know too well."

He pulled his horse back. "Come on, Cloud, if you're joining up with us. We'll catch fresh horses out of that timber and go on after the Indians."

Cloud said, "Right, sir." He started to salute, but he didn't know for sure how proper it would be. He'd never been in a military outfit before. He let the salute drop, and Barcroft didn't seem to notice.

Cloud paused a moment to shake Moseley's hand. "Take care of yourself, Lige. And maybe you ought to think over what the captain said. Sure, he's an educated feller, but it sounds to me like he makes sense."

"I ain't movin'," Moseley spoke calmly. "Anytime you're ridin' through, you'll find us here. Be sure you stop; we'll be tickled to see you." He glanced back at his daughter. "And don't forget what I told you about a man needin' a good woman."

"I won't forget," Cloud promised. He swung into his saddle and found Captain Barcroft already leading out. Cloud fell in at the rear of the company and looked back once, waving his hand.

The girl Samantha waved back.

Two

WAVING HIS HAND IN A CIRCULAR MOTION, CAPTAIN Barcroft called to his men, "Fan out and catch fresh horses. Leave the ones you have. We'll round them all up when we come back."

He moved hurriedly, yet without excitement.

It didn't take long. Some of the men formed loops in their stake ropes and cast them over horses' heads. Others, who couldn't rope, rode up beside loose horses and dropped the end of the rope over an animal's neck, then reached down and caught the rope end from beneath and drew it up, making a loop. Most of the men took some care in their selection of remounts. A few had no real idea what to look for.

Watching a few like these, Cloud thought he could understand the captain's bitterness over some of the new men. These were not frontiersmen. Men like these were the shirkers, here to keep out of war.

Cloud left his sorrel and caught a good-looking brown that had strong legs and a deep chest and looked as if it could hold out in a long run. He knew the brand on its hip. It belonged to a ranch far to the south and east. Quite a circle these Comanches had made.

In moments the men were mounted. Barcroft signaled to the Mexican, who struck out in the lead, following the trail of the Comanches.

Cloud looked around him as he rode, appraising these other members of the Texas Mounted Rifles. There was no uniform. Every man dressed as suited him—or more likely, as he could afford. Money was scarce in Texas, and always had been. Some wore homespun, some wore store cloth. A few wore buckskin. Some had high-topped, flat-heeled boots, and several wore shoes.

Cloud had seen a copy of the orders setting up a regiment of the Rifles. It required that each man should have a Colt six-shooter, if possible, plus a good double-barreled shotgun or short rifle "if convenient." He was supposed to have a half-gallon tin canteen, covered with cloth, and a good heavy blanket to sleep on.

Every man Cloud saw had a pistol on his hip. And as per orders, each carried either a shotgun or rifle across his saddle. The rifle was good for distance, but a shotgun was unbeatable in close combat. The state didn't furnish the armament. In this outfit a man brought his own weapons or didn't join.

A grinning young man with rust-red hair edged over next to Cloud and stuck out his hand. "Guffey's my name. Quade Guffey."

Cloud took his hand. "Sam Houston Cloud."

Quade made no remark about the name. It was not unusual for boys in that day to be named after General Sam. "Captain there, he gave you a pretty stiff initiation speech, but don't let it worry you. You get used to him after a while."

"You do?"

"Yep, and then you hate him even worse."

The riders passed the horse Cloud had dropped out from under one of the Comanches. Minutes later they went by the spot from which he had stampeded the herd. Cloud rode off to one side to look. He found a spot of blood where the buck had fallen, but the body was gone.

One less hole for Lige's boys to dig.

The men settled into a long trot, occasionally pushing the horses into an easy lope for a way, then pulling them down again. The Indians had a long start. But they had been pushing their horses hard when they left. The mounts would inevitably tire. By conserving their own horses all they could, the Rifles had a better chance of catching up.

Cloud soon found himself riding near the lead. It was not his way to bring up the rear. Barcroft glanced at him, appraising Cloud and his equipment. But the captain had nothing to say. He glanced toward the sun every so often, measuring the rate of its descent. Cloud knew what the man was thinking. They'd better catch those Indians before dark. Give the Comanche horses a few hours of rest and they would be as fresh again as the ones the Texans rode.

The tracks freshened. The Indians were slowing down. The Rifles came upon a horse, its throat cut. Exhausted, and killed by the Comanches so the white men couldn't get any use from him.

A little later the Mexican up front signaled and pointed to the ground. Riding up, Cloud saw the stiffening body of the Indian he had shot. It lay in the buffalo grass, abandoned by tiring Comanches who could no longer carry it.

"Crowding them," Barcroft said matter-of-factly to

those near enough to hear him. "They're getting desperate when they leave their dead."

He raised his hand and gave the signal for a speedup. Then he spurred into an easy lope and overtook the Mexican scout before the scout knew of the order.

To the west, the sun was rapidly sinking into a latticework of dry summer clouds, pretty to look at but devoid of rain. The pursuit had broken out of the brushy country and onto the open grassland that rolled for mile upon unbroken mile, toward the faraway escarpment of the Llano Estacado—the Staked Plains. Here and there a scattering of mesquites stood in low areas where the rainwater tended to run together, and the shadows of these trees were lengthening, reaching across the grass prairie like grasping fingers.

Ahead lay a creek, lined with brush. Barcroft raised his hand for a slowdown while the scout moved out to look it over. He was almost to the scrubby oaks when a rifle exploded. The ball missed the scout and sang by the men behind him. The Mexican spurred his horse sharply to the left, hitting the brush a hundred yards upstream from the source of the shot. Cloud could hear pistol fire.

Barcroft veered the command sharply to one side, upstream from the scout. When he hit the brush, he reined downstream and spurred out. Thus the Texans outflanked the Indian rear guard. Ahead of him Cloud saw the Mexican scout on one knee, aiming a six-shooter. He fired once, then the Rifles swept by him, yelping, and the scout almost lost his horse in the excitement.

Four warriors had been left in the creekbed to slow the pursuit. Two of them fired rifles, then threw the rifles down and began to run. Two others stood their ground, loosing arrows as quickly as they could pull them from deer-hide quivers and draw the bows. Cloud heard a horse go down, the rider cursing as he slid on his belly through the grass.

The Indian stand was hopeless. The troops swept over the warriors like a storm wave breaking over a lakeshore. Within the span of thirty seconds, all four Comanches lay dead. A couple of young recruits were gathering up bows and arrows as souvenirs. More practical, a pair of older men recovered the Indians' two rifles and relieved the bodies of shot and powder.

Barcroft turned in the saddle and looked back upstream. Here came the Mexican scout. He was flanked by two other riders who had held back from the battle and now rode in white-faced and shaken.

Barcroft gave his first attention to the Mexican. "Are you all right, Miguel?" The Mexican nodded. Then Barcroft faced the other two. They seemed to shrink, even before the captain spoke to them.

"What were you doing back there? Why didn't you stay up with me?"

One of the men stammered. "W-w-we thought we'd better help Miguel."

"He didn't need any help. You were trying to stay back out of the fight!" Face cloudy, Barcroft shook his fist at the two. "There's one thing in this world I hate worse than a Comanche, and that's a coward. Next time we're engaged, I'm going to see to it that you two are right up in front, or I'll shoot you myself! Is that clear?"

The two only nodded and looked at the ground.

Barcroft turned away from them. "Anybody hit?" he queried. One man had a flesh wound; nothing serious. A couple of men were out catching an Indian mount for the man whose horse had gone down. The Mexican scout was on the ground with a Bowie knife, grimly scalping the dead warriors. He held up a bloody scalp and shook it. It jingled.

"Looky there, Captain," one of the other men said, "got little bells tied in it. Ain't that the funniest thing you ever seen?"

Cloud didn't see much funny in it and turned away.

"Come on," Barcroft said impatiently, "we've lost time enough."

As scout, Miguel Soto was supposed to take the lead, but Barcroft was crowding him now in his restless haste, staying close behind him. Cloud rode almost abreast of the captain. He could see excitement building in Barcroft's face now—an eager anticipation.

Moments before sundown they spotted the Indians, strung out in a long, tired line. There were more than Cloud had supposed when he had first looked down at Moseley's, and he was doubly glad he hadn't fired into them instead of merely running off the horses. The Indians saw the pursuit and began whipping up their horses. At the distance Cloud knew most of the stragglers were squaws. Some of the bucks began dropping back to protect them, but some were trying to get on out ahead, even at the expense of the squaws.

Most Comanches took pains to protect their women and children, but once Cloud had seen a warrior pull a squaw down off a horse and take it for his own getaway. They could be as cold-blooded about it as some white men.

Ahead lay a stretch of oak timber.

"Spur out, men," Barcroft shouted. "If they make that brush, and dark coming on, we'll lose them."

He used his leather quirt. The riders with the best horses began pulling forward in a ragged line. Those on poorer mounts, and those who didn't really want to be in the thick of it, began falling back. Barcroft looked behind him, searching out the men who had held back in the last skirmish. "You two—Holmes, Ulbrich—get yourselves up here and fight! Spur up, I tell you, or I'll have you shot!''

Somehow the two got extra speed out of their horses.

Their mounts fresher, the Rifles rapidly closed the distance between themselves and the Indians. A few of the newer men wasted a long shot or two that picked up dust far from the Comanches.

Barcroft shouted, ''Hold your fire till you can hit something.'' He used the quirt some more.

One of the warriors stopped his horse suddenly, reined about and raised a rifle. It spat fire. The man named Ulbrich screamed and tumbled from the saddle. Barcroft didn't even look back. Pistol in his hand, he bore down on the Indian and pulled the trigger. The Indian fell. Galloping by, other men fired at the Comanche, making sure he was dead.

From here on it was an easy butchery until the lead Indians got into the brush and scattered like quail. One fell, then another and another. Spurring past, Cloud looked down at one broken body and realized it was a squaw. Regret gripped him, but he knew there was no sense in worrying about it. In a running fight, it was sometimes hard to tell a squaw from a buck.

As Moseley had said, *she just ortn't to've been there.*

The sun was gone, the dusk quickly deepening. The troops were far into the brush, and firing had stopped. The Indians had vanished. His horse sweat-lathered and breathing hard, Barcroft called out, ''Assemble! Pass the word, assemble!''

Cloud reined in beside the captain and took the opportunity to reload his six-shooter. His breath was short from the hard run, and his heart was thumping from the excitement. He looked at the captain and saw the man's chest heaving. Barcroft was almost out of breath, yet there was exultation in his face. Pleasure showed in his black eyes as he looked down upon the body of a Comanche warrior.

The Mexican scout dismounted and said, "With your permission, *Capitán*?" He had his knife out and ready.

Barcroft said, "Help yourself."

Something cold passed through Cloud as he watched. Barcroft caught the look. "Bother you, Cloud?"

"Can't say as I like it."

"Indians scalp their victims, or don't you know?"

"They're savages. We're white men."

"We're fighting a savage foe, Cloud. If we're to survive, we need to become as savage as he is."

"Can't say as I accept that, Captain."

Firmly Barcroft said, "*I* accept it, and I'm the captain here."

Cloud glanced sharply at him but said nothing more.

The men gathered and took count of each other, anxious to know if friends had made it through all right. Only one man was lost—Ulbrich. He wasn't much of a loss, Cloud heard Quade Guffey remark. It had been a one-sided fight. Barcroft eyed his men with satisfaction. He turned to the scout Miguel. "How many would you say got away?"

Miguel Soto shrugged. "Ten, maybe. Mostly squaws. The bucks, they try to fight and we pretty much kill."

"Do you think the survivors are heading for an encampment, a rendezvous of some kind ahead?"

"*Quién sabe, mi capitán?*" Soto shrugged again. "Somewhere up yonder, more Indians come together, I think. Most of the time these bands they split up to make the raids. Later they meet somewhere in this open country, where the white man don' go. The little bands they make one pretty good-sized band. They sing and dance and celebrate. Then they all go home together."

"And where is home?"

"Far. Very far, yonder," he said, pointing northward,

and a little west. "Up there, no white man ever go."

Barcroft stood a moment chewing his lip, looking northward into the dusk, a wish in his black eyes. "Someday," he murmured. "Someday . . ."

He finally turned back to his men. "We'll move out of this brush while we can still see. First light of day, we'll start again, following tracks. If there's an encampment up yonder, and it's not too big for us to handle, we'll kill us some more Indians."

Soto frowned. "*Mi capitán,* maybeso it *is* too big. Then what we do?"

Barcroft said evenly, "You men will do what I tell you. And I'll do whatever looks best at the time."

The company stopped at the edge of the brush to build fires and make coffee. Some of the men had dried beef to eat, and some broiled bacon on sticks. After supper they would move on, camping for the night in another spot well away from the glow of dying embers, the possible scrutiny of Comanche eyes.

Captain Barcroft never really relaxed. While the other men prepared their supper, he strode restlessly among them, looking them over, searching for no-one-knew-what. Finally a man named Elkin motioned to him, and Barcroft went to Elkin's fire, where Elkin had prepared a little supper for the two of them.

Cloud took Elkin to be Barcroft's second-in-command, although nothing had been said about it. Elkin was a quiet, blocky man well into his forties, a man who went about his business with a quiet competence. Here was a man, Cloud thought, who knew what he was doing and didn't seem to feel he had to prove it to anybody. Elkin had stayed right up front in the running skirmish. A time or two when Barcroft was at some distance, Cloud had seen Elkin give signal commands to some of the other troopers, and they had taken them.

Barcroft quickly ate his beef and drank his black coffee, as if eating was a chore to be disposed of as hurriedly as possible. That done, he stretched his long legs out in the curing grass and took from his pocket the letter Cloud had given him. He held it down close to Elkin's small mesquite-wood fire and read it in the flickering flame light. With a nod of his head he motioned Cloud to come to him and sit down.

"Letter says you know this country, Cloud."

Cloud shook his head. "Not very well, but I've been over part of it. Had me some cows in the country a little east of here. Comanches ran most of them off, and I rode over a lot of this area here huntin' for 'em."

"Find them?"

"No, sir. About all I found was experience. It just about finished me in the cow business."

Barcroft's chin pointed to the letter. "The colonel says here you can track, read signs and know something about Indians. He thinks you'd make a scout if the company needed you for that."

Cloud said, "I didn't read the letter."

"Miguel could use some help, all right. We had another scout but lost him in an ambush. Indian rose up out of the tall grass and put an arrow so deep into the scout's belly that the point came out of his back. Do you want the job?"

Don't sound like there's much of a future to it, Cloud thought. But this day in time a man didn't get a lot of choice. "You're the captain."

Barcroft had a stern gaze that made a man fidgety, made him want to get out from under it. "You've worried me a little, Cloud. I watched you in action today, and you made a good account of yourself. You didn't strike me as a glory hunter, or as a shirker either. It doesn't take long to tell the counterfeits. I gathered you're not here because you're afraid to fight the Yankees. Then you must be here because you don't *want* to fight them. I'd like to know your politics, mister. Are you a damned Unionist?"

Uncomfortable, Cloud studied a moment before he tried to answer. "I'm a Texican, Captain. I was born here in '36, durin' the Runaway Scrape. My ma, she had to drop out of a bunch of refugees on account of me, and I was born just a few miles ahead of old Santa Anna and his Mexican troops. My folks always thought of themselves as Americans, and they were tickled to death when Texas was annexed. That's the way I was brought up.

"Sure, I'm a Southerner, and I think the Yankees have done us a heap of wrong. I think we got some scores to settle with them. But war ain't no proper way to go about it. You boil it down, Captain, they're white folks same as us. They're Americans, and so are we—whatever we might be callin' ourselves right now. I got to agree with old General Sam Houston, that secession was one mighty bad mistake. There must've been a better way out than goin' to war against our own people.

"If there's fightin' to be done, I won't shirk my share of it. But I'll do mine here, at the edge of the settlements, where there's an enemy I can recognize as one."

Cloud could see anger in the captain's face. "A lot of people in Texas seem to feel the way you do. Some have even slipped off and joined the Union Army."

Cloud shook his head. "That'd be even worse. Far as I'm concerned, this war is a mistake for both sides. I don't want none of it, either way."

Barcroft said, "If the yellow-leg Yankee cavalry had ever done to you what it did to me, you'd think differently. I'd be up yonder fighting them now, except that they need somebody to do this, and I hate Comanches even more than Yankees."

He stood up, and Cloud followed suit. Gravely Barcroft

said: "Normally, a man's entitled to think as he pleases, Cloud. But this is wartime, and in wartime a man has to forgo a lot of rights. There are several in this command who have the same Unionist ideas you do. If you and the others weren't so badly needed here, you'd probably be hanged. So just remember this: you're in the Confederacy, like it or not. Keep your ideas to yourself and we'll get along. But I'll allow no traitorous talk in this command!"

He turned away and said to Elkin, "Let's move!"

By the time first sunlight spilled out across the dry prairie, the company had eaten its meager breakfast and was a-horseback again. Barcroft motioned to Cloud and pointed forward.

"You go up with Miguel and help him scout."

Cloud nodded and spurred his horse into a lope, overtaking the Mexican well forward of the command. Miguel Soto looked him over as he rode up. "The man who steals horses so good," Soto said, a trace of a smile about him. The Mexican was short and wiry and all muscle. He was not an old man, but Cloud could not make even a wild guess at his age. He rather thought Soto was young, although his face was weathered. A long scar down one cheek helped give him the appearance of age.

Cloud had watched the Mexican with some wonder last night. The other Texans had treated Soto as one of themselves. There had been no sign of resentment or dislike. Most Texans of that day cared little for Mexicans, for they had been enemies in two wars and countless border skirmishes, and even a Texas-born Mexican was likely to be regarded as an alien. That the group here so readily accepted Soto indicated he had already proved himself.

"Maybeso the *capitán*, he don't like you," Soto commented with a grin. "Maybeso he send you up here to get kill, eh?"

Cloud saw little to grin about, but he tried it anyway. ''Don't look to me like you're in any place to smile. You're up here too.''

Soto shrugged. ''Long time now the Comanche, he has try to kill Miguel. But I have live with the Comanche. I know how he thinks, what he's gonna do. This Mexican, he gonna die in bed, a long time from now.''

The sun was still low in the east, and a cool morning breeze searched across the rolling prairie as if seeking a place of refuge from the coming heat. Cloud and Soto passed the spot where they had fixed supper the night before, the burned-out campfires only spots of gray ash amid the carpet of short grass. They cut the trail left by themselves and by the Indians in yesterday's running fight. Here and there lay a stiffened horse, a dead Indian. Cloud shuddered. This was something a man never got used to.

Soto stepped down to recover a bow and a quiver of arrows.

''You don't look to me like a souvenir hunter,'' Cloud remarked.

Soto shook his head. ''I already got my Comanche souvenir,'' he said, pointing to the long scar on his face. ''But maybeso we come to a place where we got to kill quiet, and don' want no gun. The arrow, she don't make much noise.''

Suddenly Cloud reined up and pointed. ''Miguel, look yonder.''

An Indian woman was dragging herself along in the grass, trying to crawl away from them. A hundred feet behind her lay a blanket and a blood-splotched patch of ground where she had fallen in the skirmish.

''Must've laid there all night,'' Cloud said.

They rode up to her carefully. Cloud held his pistol ready. It wasn't likely the squaw would have a gun, but it was foolish to take chances. Miguel unstrapped his canteen and stepped down. He spoke to the woman in the Comanche tongue. She stopped crawling and turned over on her side. Hatred shone through the pain in her dark eyes.

Cloud put the pistol away and swung to the ground. The woman was young. It might have been the squaw who was sitting beside the buck he had shot yesterday, at the horse herd.

Miguel held his canteen out to her. She refused it at first. Miguel took the lid off and let a little of the water trickle out into the grass. The woman's reserve broke. She clutched at the canteen. Talking quietly to her, Miguel held it for her while she drank thirstily.

Cloud dropped to one knee and looked at the shoulder wound that had brought her down. He gritted his teeth and turned away.

Afraid she was drinking too rapidly, Miguel withheld the canteen a moment. She begged for it, and he let her drink again. Fever, Cloud thought. She's all dried out.

The rest of the company caught up to them, Captain Barcroft in the lead. He asked no foolish questions. He stared at the woman without either hatred or pity.

Cloud said, "Looks like this complicates things, Captain. Was we just to leave her here like this, she'd die."

The captain said, "She's obviously in no condition to go anywhere, either afoot or on horseback. We couldn't take her with us."

"We could leave a man to take care of her till we come back."

"Leave a man out here alone, with other Indians possibly about? Besides, Cloud, we can't spare anyone—not even one man. We don't know what we'll run into up yonder."

Cloud nodded. "Sir, this is a woman. I don't see any other way out."

Evenly Barcroft said, "There's a way out, Cloud. A very simple way."

Cloud froze in shocked disbelief as Barcroft drew his pistol and leveled it at the woman. He saw terror in the squaw's brown eyes, and he shouted, "Don't!"

The pistol flashed and the woman fell back. Cloud dropped to one knee beside her. But he knew at a glance that she was dead. Trembling in rage, he slowly pushed to his feet and turned to face the captain. He felt a strong impulse to drag the man out of the saddle, but he knew that could get him shot. He struggled for words, and they wouldn't come.

Barcroft said, "Don't say anything that'll get you in trouble, Cloud. When you think about it a little, you'll know it was the best way out for her and for us. Now go on, you and Miguel. Take up your positions again."

Cloud glared at him through a red haze, his fists doubled.

"Cloud!" Barcroft spoke again, a sharpness in his voice this time. "Don't ask for trouble. You heard my order."

Miguel tugged at Cloud's sleeve. "You better do what he says, my friend."

Cloud lingered a moment more, his eyes still burning on the captain. But the quick blaze of anger died down in him, leaving a smoldering coal that would turn into hatred. He pivoted on one heel and swung into the saddle. He spurred out in a lope.

Three

AS THE SUN CLIMBED, THE SUMMER HEAT BORE DOWN unmercifully. Cloud sweated hard, his shirt sticking to his back. The wind itself turned warm, but now and again it felt pleasant as it made the wet shirt cool against his skin. In this country there was nearly always a little wind through the daytime. Without it, the sun would be almost unbearable.

The surviving Indians had ridden far into the night. Finally, they had paused to rest a little while, starting again by daylight. At first they had made no effort to conceal their tracks. Now their panic was subsiding. Judgment was getting the upper hand. They were covering their trail.

Cloud was a good tracker. As a boy he had developed the art from trailing lost cattle and horses, and he had learned to watch for Indian signs. But now and again he would lose the Comanches' trail. Miguel Soto always found something to set the pair of scouts right again.

"You follow them like another Indian," Cloud observed in admiration.

"I *was* an Indian. The Comanches, they make me one."

"How's that?"

"Long time ago, when I was a boy in Chihuahua, the Comanches come. I am eight, maybeso ten years old. They kill my mother and father and my big brothers, strike them down with their lances and their arrows. With these two eyes, I see them take the scalps. The two sisters I have, the young warriors carry them away. My baby brother and me, some others take us along. The baby, he cry all the time, so they smash his head on a rock. Me, I am strong and healthy, and they keep me to work.

"It is a hard life, I tell you. They beat me all the time. Even now, I have on my back the many scars. But I don' cry. Sometimes when they beat me I fight, and they like that. All the time I work hard, so they don' kill me, and I tell myself someday I get my chance. Someday I will get even with them for what they do to me, to all my people.

"Finally they decide I make pretty good Comanche myself, and they don' beat me no more. They raise me like Comanche boy, teach me what they teach all Comanche boys. They think I forget all the bad things, but I don' forget. I all the time remember, and I tell myself—wait, one day the time will come.

"Sure enough, when I get to the age, we go on big raid against the *Tejanos.* This is my chance. The old warrior who always beat me the most, he is there. I get him alone, and I cut his throat." Soto made the sign with his finger, and grinned with a grim satisfaction as he did so. "I laugh at him and I spit on him while he is lie there, lookin' up at me and dyin'. Then I take coup. I still have the scalp."

He reached back into his saddlebag and drew forth a piece of rolled-up oilskin. He unrolled it and showed

Cloud a scalp, tanned to keep. "This," said Miguel, "I keep with me always, so I don' never forget. Here, feel of it. Good piece of work, eh?"

Face twisting, Cloud shook his head. "I'll take your word for it."

Miguel rolled the scalp back into the oilskin. "Sometimes when I go into battle against the Comanche, I think of some of the boys who were good to me, and I begin to feel sorry. Then I look at this scalp and remember all the bad things, and I don't feel sorry no more. I got plenty to hate for."

He frowned then, looking back over his shoulder at Barcroft's company, far behind them. "My friend, there is much you don' know about the *capitán.* You think he is a bad man, and maybeso he is, a little bit. But it is not because he wants to be. He is like me—he has much to hate for. *Quién sabe?* Maybeso one day you understand."

Cloud said sharply, "Some things, there ain't no understandin'."

All that day they rode without once sighting an Indian. But they came across Indian signs, tracks headed north. There were the hoofprints of many horses, even the trail of travois. No longer was there any apparent effort by the Comanches to hide their tracks. This was farther than *Tejano* pursuit usually came. Ahead, for the Indians, lay unviolated sanctuary.

Only once all day did the company come across a waterhole. Barcroft and Elkin saw to it that every canteen was filled before the horses were allowed to move in and water.

"Every man should drink up good while he's here," Barcroft said, wiping the sweat from his face. "Conserve that canteen water as long as you can. No telling how long before we find more."

Grudgingly, Cloud admitted to himself that the captain's order was a wise one. Men had ridden out horseback on searches into the open Indian country, only to drag back to the settlements on hands and knees, tongues swollen, lips parched, begging for water.

Through the heat of the afternoon they rode on, but slowly now, for Barcroft was trying to save the horses. These mounts would have to get them to wherever they were going and carry them home again. From here on, there was likely to be no chance for a change.

Late in the day they came upon a dry creekbed lined by a scrubby growth of brush and dying grass. Cloud dismounted and poked around, shoving his ramrod deep into the bed and drawing it out. He felt the rod and found mud clinging to the end of it. "Been water here," he said. "I expect if we was to dig holes in it, we could water the horses by mornin' from what seeps in."

Spotting a cottontail rabbit, the Mexican took down the bow he had picked up earlier. The captain had given orders against gunfire. With the first arrow, Soto pinned the rabbit to the ground. Cloud whistled. "They sure taught you good."

"Supper," said Soto, holding up the rabbit. "We share it, you and me."

The company scattered up and down the dry creekbed, building tiny fires behind the banks to hide them from searching eyes. Some of the men already were complaining that they were out of meat, that it was time to turn back. Those who still had food left shared it with those whose supplies had run out.

Cloud was grateful for the rabbit, though he was still a little hungry when he finished his half of it. Cottontails didn't grow very big.

The rusty-haired young man named Quade Guffey had sat down beside Cloud to chew on a piece of cold jerky.

He enviously eyed the rabbit, cooking over a small bank of coals, but he refused Cloud's offer to split his share with him.

"Ain't hardly enough there for *you,*" Guffey said. "Man in this outfit gets used to the lank days anyhow. Trouble with this Indian-huntin' ain't so much the danger you run into once in a while. It's the meals you miss and all the times you go thirsty because the waterhole you counted on was dried up, or it wasn't where you thought it was after all. Feller learns after a while to do like the Indian does—stuff your gut when you can get it, and don't go complainin' when you can't."

Guffey had such a happy-go-lucky attitude about it all that Cloud was curious. "How'd you come to join this outfit, Guffey?"

"Been wonderin' myself." He grinned. "The call went out, and I asked myself what the hell. Spent my whole life workin' for the other feller anyhow, ridin' the other man's horse, plowin' the other man's field. Figured here was a chance to get a little fresh air, be where the noise was bein' made, maybe shoot me an Indian. And git paid for it too."

The grin faded. "There was somethin' else. I knew that pretty soon they'd come callin' for me to go fight them Yankees. I had the same feelin's on that score that you did." To Cloud's questioning glance, Guffey explained, "I heard what you told the captain last night. I was curious about you, so I plopped myself down where I could listen. I don't want to shoot no Yankees. Far as I'm concerned, this is a rich man's war, only they want the poor man to do all the fightin'. My folks never had nothin'. I never owned a slave and never will, so it ain't no skin off my nose if Abe Lincoln wants to take the slaves away. Might even make a poor white man's wages better. But these rich plantation folks, they want us to fight and keep their slaves for them. Way I see it, if they want to fight, let 'em do it theirselves."

Cloud looked about to see if the captain was within earshot. He wasn't. "Guffey, there's a sight more to it than just slaves."

"Not as far as I'm concerned there ain't. They make a heap of fine talk about other things I don't even understand, but all I see in it is slaves."

That's the way it is these days, Cloud thought. *Most people look at it head-on and make up their minds one way or the other. Secession or union. Slave or free. White or black, and no compromise between.*

He wished it could be that simple for him. He had pondered over it a long time before he had made his choice. Even after he chose, he continued to worry about it, wondering if he was right. He still wondered, sometimes.

Without knowing why, he wanted to argue with Guffy now, and he realized his argument would be in favor of the Confederacy.

Who can say what's right and wrong, he asked himself, *when there's so much argument to make for either side?*

Morning, and restlessness stirred the company. The water that had seeped into the holes dug in the creekbed was so muddy the men couldn't drink it, and most of the horses wouldn't either. Some of the canteens were nearly empty, and many men were out of food. A few of the horses picked up in the brush at Moseley's had not proved out.

The company had discipline enough that the men would take orders from Barcroft. But it was not so strongly disciplined that they wouldn't give him their advice. These were free men. A majority had lived on the frontier, or not far back from it. They thought for themselves and said what they thought. Barcroft listened patiently enough to their complaints, but gave no sign that he was convinced. He walked up to Miguel Soto.

"What do you think, Miguel? Are we close to an Indian camp?"

Miguel frowned. "Who can say? By the signs, I think maybeso."

"How big would you say it might be?"

"That, *mi capitán*, I cannot say at all. The sign say pretty soon now the Indians come together. Maybe many, maybe not so very many. We see when we see."

That didn't satisfy the captain, but it was all he could get. He glanced a moment at Cloud as if expecting Cloud to offer advice too. All he got from Cloud was a half-hostile stare. Barcroft turned back to his graying lieutenant, Elkin.

"We've gone this far. It's wasted unless we go a little farther."

"What will we gain, Captain?"

"We can kill some more Indians."

Elkin said, "There may not be any water ahead, and there's little chance of food. It'll be a long, dry, hungry trip back out."

Barcroft replied, "Any man who thinks this is too hard on him can ask to join the Confederate Army instead. Maybe he'll like Virginia better."

He gave the signal for mounting up, then motioned for Cloud and Soto to ride out first.

This was a hotter day than yesterday. Even early, the sun began to blister. Cloud nursed his half canteen of water carefully, afraid it might have to last a long time. He tipped it up, taking just enough water to wet his lips and tongue. Later he put a pebble in his mouth and kept it there. It helped, some.

Looking behind him at the company, he could see it straggling out.

"Captain's goin' to lose half the command if he don't make 'em close it up," he said to Soto. "Better still, he ought to call a halt."

"He is a stubborn man."

"Stubbornness won't take the place of food and water and fresh horses."

Earnestly, Soto said, "Stubbornness takes the place of many things."

Cloud's eyebrows lifted. "Every time I say somethin' about him, you take up for him. You really believe in the captain, don't you?"

"Up to now, the *capitán* he never disappoint me. Until he disappoint me, I believe in him."

The noon stop was made on schedule, but it was more for rest than anything else. Little food was left among the Rifles. Those who still had it shared it among the others. The captain gave all of his own food away, not eating anything. He roamed around looking at his men, surveying their horses. His dark eyes were restless, his face sad beneath a covering of dust, a growth of black beard.

Studying Barcroft, Cloud sensed a driving urgency about the man. There was a devil in him someplace, a black torment that would not leave him be.

Elkin finished the little he had to eat, then stepped up beside Barcroft. "I'm afraid the company's about finished, Captain." He said it with the gentle manner of an older man trying to give advice to a younger one without being insistent. "There's not another day left in them."

Barcroft looked off to the north. "Perhaps not a day. Then *half* a day. Surely we can get that much out of them."

"We've got to save something for the trip back."

Barcroft shook his head. "The trip back will take care of itself. A man on his way home can always find the strength to keep going a little longer. The hard part is this, the search."

Cloud heard complaining as the captain pointed the scouts ahead after the noon rest. But looking back, he saw the captain silently ride out, his grim eyes fixed straight ahead. And the whole command followed him.

Cloud said, "I don't know how he can keep drivin' 'em on."

Soto replied, "He don' drive them, my friend. He *leads* them."

The smell of woodsmoke was the first sign. Cloud and Soto caught it at the same time, and they reined up to sniff the wind.

"There's water up yonder someplace," Cloud said. "You notice how them buffalo trails been anglin' closer together all the time? They're pointin' in to water like wheel spokes point to the hub."

Miguel nodded. "Water and smoke. And Comanches."

Cloud squinted, but he could see nothing ahead except the continuing roll of the brown-grass hills. As the two men waited for the company to come up, their horses began to paw impatiently. They smelled water.

The captain had caught the scent by the time he reached the scouts. His shoulders had squared, and an eager light began to show in his eyes. He ran his tongue over dry, cracked lips. The solid grip of confidence was in his dusty face.

"Where there's a village, there's bound to be water," he said.

Dourly, Cloud reminded him, "And there's bound to be Indians."

The captain ignored Cloud's dislike of him. "I'll hold the men here out of sight while you two go on and scout out the village. See how the camp is laid out. Try to estimate how many Comanches there are. And Miguel . . ." The Mexican lifted his chin to listen. "Miguel, see if there are children."

Cloud asked, "What if there's too many Indians for us, Captain? We've got awful close to water to turn back now."

"Sometimes you just have to depend upon Providence."

"Providence is all right," Cloud responded dryly, "but I'd rather depend on somethin' I can see a little plainer."

Together the two rode out while the Rifles dismounted to rest their horses and check their guns. Like the captain, the men showed a lift to their shoulders, a new vitality that had come from within. The smell of water had even perked up the horses a little.

Cloud and Soto rode into the wind, rifles balanced across their laps. Soto had the bow ready, too, the quiver slung across his shoulder Indian-style. They angled between the gently rolling hills the best they could, trying to avoid being skylined. An Indian could tell the look of a *Tejano* hat almost as far as he could see the rider.

The smoke smell became stronger. The two men passed between two hills and found a line of brush leading out through a summer-parched swale. Cloud nodded toward it, and they silently edged into the brush for cover. A horse nickered somewhere ahead. Cloud's horse almost answered, and Cloud had to drop quickly to the ground and stop him. He stood there a moment after it was all over, still gripping the animal's nose, his heart high in his throat. He looked up at the grinning Mexican and tried to say something, but it wasn't there. Cloud wiped the cold sweat from his face as the tension slowly ran out of him.

Soto swung down, the bow in his hand. He and Cloud led their horses through the brush, careful to make no noise. Finally they could see the village ahead. There were twenty-five or thirty buffalo-skin tepees, strung out down a green-banked little creek fed by a spring somewhere above. The openings all faced east, away from the afternoon sun. Smoke curled from several outdoor fires, for in this hot weather the cooking was being done outside. Under a scattering of brush arbors, the bucks and most of the squaws loafed in the shade. Children played under the arbors and around the tepees. A few splashed in the creek.

"It's quiet down there," Cloud observed. "Maybe too hot for them to stir much. Don't look like a very happy camp to me."

"Those Indians we chase, they bring bad news. This is a waitin' camp. Here is where the raidin' bands, they split up to go south. Squaws and children, they mostly stay here. A few young squaws, they go to watch. Later on, the raiders meet here again. I think not all the bands have come back."

"How many fightin' bucks you reckon is in that camp?"

Soto squinted as he gazed off in the direction of the pony herd, loose-held down the creek by a couple of young boys who loafed in the shade, their own horses cropping the green grass of the creekbank.

"Hard to say, except by the pony herd. Not too many for us, I think."

Brush crackled behind them. They whirled, wide-eyed. They saw a Comanche warrior at the moment he saw them. Afoot, he had a bow and arrow and a string of three or four dead rabbits he was taking into camp. For just a moment he stared in surprise. Then he opened his mouth to shout.

Cloud brought up his six-shooter but realized suddenly he could not afford to shoot. He saw a blur of movement from Soto, then heard the slap of a bowstring, the solid plunk of Soto's arrow driving into the warrior's body.

Instead of the shout, there was only a groan. The Comanche sank to the grass and died.

Quickly Cloud looked back toward the village again, sweat breaking on his forehead. There had been little noise, and he doubted that it had carried to the camp. But you never knew. . . .

He saw no change in the village, no sign anyone had heard. Not even a dog barked.

Soto motioned for him to pull back. Cloud took one last wishful glance at the creek. "I'd give my eyeteeth for a drink of that cool water."

"And your hair too?"

It took a while to get back to the company. Miguel briefly told the captain what they had seen. Cloud could see the men's faces light up as Soto told about the creek, about the racks of meat they had seen drying.

"Nocona band, you say?" the captain spoke. "And you saw women and children in the camp?" Cloud saw anxiety in the man's eyes.

"*Sí, Capitán.*"

Barcroft's hands trembled a little. He turned to the men who had gathered up close around him. "There's one order I want all of you to hear. I don't want any of those children hurt, do you understand? Not under any circumstances. If you have to pass up a shot at a warrior to keep from hitting a child, then pass it. And as we charge in, take every pain to keep from running a horse over a child. Is that understood?"

He turned back to the Mexican scout. "Now, then, let's draw a plan of that village here in the dirt." Soto did, with help from Cloud, who otherwise had said nothing and offered nothing.

The captain nodded over the crude map. He glanced up at the sun. "We'll have to get on with it to be finished and out of here before dark. But it doesn't look too difficult, so long as we can take them by surprise."

He glanced up at Cloud. "You seem to be good at stampeding horses. I want you to take a couple of men and run off that horse herd. That's for diversion. Make plenty of noise. It'll draw the warriors out into the open. The rest of us will work around the other end and outflank the village. As you hit the herd and the bucks come running out, we'll ride in and make a fast, clean sweep straight down the line of tepees. A minute or two, that's all it should take. I want every warrior dead."

He stood up and looked around him. "When that's done, we'll go back and circle the village. Chances are the women and children will scatter like quail. I want them rounded up and brought back in, all of them."

Cloud stiffened. In a hostile voice he demanded, "What you aimin' to do, Captain, shoot all the squaws?"

Barcroft's eyes flamed. For a moment Cloud thought the captain was going to hit him. He wished the man would.

Crisply Barcroft said, "You were sent here under my command, Cloud; don't you forget that. What I did yesterday was out of necessity. I don't kill squaws unless I have to."

"But you don't seem to mind doin' it." He turned away from the captain. "Guffey, how about you comin' with me? Bring somebody you know."

The three split away from the company and followed the route Cloud and Soto had reconnoitered. The last part of the way they made afoot, carefully working down into the brush overlooking the village. The horse herd was still where it had been, and the same two boys were watching it. But now the sun had lost some of its heat, and the boys were out in the open, sliding up and down on their gentle ponies' backs.

Cloud said, "We'll wait a spell, give the others time

enough to get ready. I'd hate to ride off in there and find out I was by myself."

Guffey was hungrily eyeing a meat rack down in the camp. "I just hope some fool don't ride a horse into that rack and spill all the meat."

Guffey had brought along a boy of seventeen or eighteen named Tommy Sides. The youngster was not old enough to have grown any whiskers of account during the days of march. He said, "Guffey, that there's Indian meat. Flies been all over it. You mean to tell me you'd actually eat that stuff?"

"Boy," said Guffey, "if I was hungry enough, I'd eat the Indian hisself."

The boy swallowed, wondering whether to believe it. Cloud smiled. The kid was green, but he had nerve. He was putting up a brave front even though he was light-skinned and suffered terribly from sunburn. There were some who said this Texas sun wasn't meant for a white man.

Finally Cloud said, "They ought to be ready by now." He brought up his rifle. "Guffey, let's you and me shoot the horses out from under them two boys yonder. Ain't no sense in hurtin' the boys. Then we'll run the horses down the creek, away from camp and out of the hands of any bucks that might get through."

He went to the end of his stake rope, as did Guffey. They leveled their rifles across tree limbs to hold them steady. "Now," said Cloud. The rifles spoke together. The two horses fell. One boy was pinned down. The other scrambled away from his kicking pony. Quickly then, Cloud and Guffey ran back to their horses, coiling the ropes as they went. They swung up and spurred out after the herd.

Four

THEY FIRED THEIR PISTOLS AND SQUALLED LOUDLY. The Indians' horses broke into a hard run down the creek. One of the herd boys was still trying to fight his way out from under his fallen pony. The other shouted angrily at Cloud. He stooped and picked up a rock, hurling it and striking Guffey's horse.

In the village, every dog was awake and barking. Men shouted. Squaws screamed. Cloud slowed and looked back over his shoulder. Comanche men came running out from under the arbors and from the tepees. A couple or three who carried rifles fired futilely at the *Tejano* horse thieves. Several braves came running afoot. Two had horses staked near their tepees. These swung up and struck out after the horse herd, short-bows in their hands.

"Guffey, Tommy, look out," Cloud shouted. He stopped his horse and wheeled about as the first of the braves came riding. Cloud's rifle was empty, for he hadn't taken time to reload. He fought his mount to a standstill, held up his left arm and steadied the pistol over it with his right. He fired and saw the Indian go down.

The kid was on the ground and running to the end of his stake rope, rifle in hand. He brought up the rifle just as the second Indian rider let loose an arrow. The arrow pierced the boy's arm and he went down with a cry of pain. Guffey turned around and stepped off his horse, grabbing up the boy's rifle. As the Indian brought down his bow for a second shot, Guffey fired. The Comanche's mount fell kicking. The arrow plunked harmlessly into the creek mud.

The Indian scrambled to his feet and grabbed up the bow. He pulled another arrow from the quiver and was fitting it to the bowstring when Cloud spurred back by him, pistol in hand. The pistol flashed. The Comanche fell.

By then, gunfire had erupted at the far end of the village. The Comanche warriors who pursued the horses afoot turned and faced the terror that came galloping at them, twenty shouting *Tejanos* with guns ablaze, sharp hoofs cutting deep into the foot-packed sod. Barcroft was in the lead, pistol spitting fire. Warrior after warrior fell beneath the savage hail of bullets.

On either side of the creek, women and children ran for the brush, screaming, crying for help. Some warriors followed suit, only to be cut down by a relentless wave of angry Texans.

Cloud saw Barcroft signal the men to swing about and circle the outside of the camp. Cloud then spurred out around the horse herd and began slowing it down. With Guffey's help he soon had the horses milling. Slowly the pair of them started the horses back toward the village.

Gunfire had stopped. The surprise had been complete. So had the victory.

As the horses came up even with the fallen kid, Cloud signaled Guffey to hold them up. Then he rode out to the boy and dismounted. Tommy Sides sat on the ground, face twisted in pain. He held the wounded arm, blood flowing out around the wooden shaft.

Cloud examined the stone arrowhead. "Went clean through." He realized the boy knew it well enough without his saying it. With a sharp bowie knife Cloud whittled the shaft off well above the head.

"Now," he said, "I'm goin' to pull it out. Yell, cuss, do anything, but just see that you hold still. It ain't goin' to be fun."

He yanked, and the bloody shaft drew out. The kid gave a sharp cry of pain, then sobbed quietly. In a moment he managed to stop. "I'm sorry," he choked. "I'm actin' like a baby."

Cloud shook his head and gripped the boy's knee with a touch of pride. "When a man hurts, he's just naturally got to make a little noise. That takes the edge off of it. Grown men cry too, so you don't need to worry over that. Now the bleedin' ought to've washed that hole clean. We got to stop it before it drains the life out of you."

He had nothing to wrap with except the handkerchief in his pocket. It was dirty, but he had to use it. He bound the wound tightly.

"Come on," he said, "I'll take you in and see if somebody's got somethin' better to do the job with." He turned back to Guffey. "Think you can hold them horses by yourself?"

Guffey nodded. "I've got 'em. You take care of the kid."

Tommy paused, despite his pain, to pick up the arrowhead and the whittled-off shaft. Something to show his grandchildren someday, if he lived to have any.

In the village, Texans were rounding up the women and

children, moving them into the center of camp. From the far side of the creek, from out of the brush, they came herding the crying squaws and squalling children like so many cattle. One Indian boy five or six years old hit a trooper in the face with a rock. The trooper swung down and grabbed up the boy. He bent him over his uplifted knee and thrashed him as he would his own.

Passing the bodies of their fallen men, the squaws would drop to their knees and begin to cry out a painful chant. The Rifles would let them carry on a moment or two, then would make them get up and go on with the others.

Cloud rode up to the captain. "We got a hurt boy. Anybody here better than average at fixin' 'em up?"

Barcroft motioned with his chin. "Back yonder somewhere. Walt Johnson's a doctor of sorts. He's taking care of the wounded."

Young Walt Johnson had his hands full. A Texan shot low in the chest lay dying on an Indian buffalo robe Johnson had spread out beneath a brush arbor. Other men with lesser wounds sat patiently waiting while Johnson gave his attention to the dying man.

Tommy Sides, pale from shock, said, "I'll make it, Mister Cloud. You don't have to worry about me no more."

Cloud touched his shoulder. "Good boy." He turned away.

By twos and threes, the men were moving up the creek to water their horses and drink a fill for themselves. One corner of the meat rack had gone down, just as Guffey had said, but most of the meat still hung above ground. The Texans were taking it. In some of the tepees they also found Indian pemmican tied up in gut casings.

Captain Barcroft looked over the group of women and children. There must have been fifty or sixty women, and even more children than that.

"Are you sure this is all of them?" he asked Elkin.

"All that've been found, Captain."

The captain turned to Miguel Soto. "Tell them to form a line. I want to look over these children."

Soto barked something in Comanche. The women were slow to comply, and he said it again, rougher this time. They strung out in a long line, clutching their children to them. Some of the women wailed as they stood there. A plaintive chant began.

"They think we shoot them, *Capitán*," Soto explained.

Barcroft nodded grimly. "They know that's what would happen if we were Comanches and they were white women. That, or worse." He stepped forward. "All right, Miguel, let's see these children."

Cloud stared in wonder as Barcroft started at one end of the line, carefully looking over the children. Seeing Elkin nearby, Cloud edged up to him and said, "What's he up to?"

"Looking for captive children," Elkin replied. "Any captives, but especially his own."

"His own?" Cloud's mouth dropped open.

Elkin nodded. "About three years or so ago, it was. The Comanches captured the captain's wife and his three-year-old daughter. He found his wife later, up the trail. She was dead." Elkin dropped his chin, staring at the ground. "He never did find his daughter. But he's still looking, Cloud, still looking."

Cloud turned back toward the tall, grim man who slowly moved down the line, examining the children. Cloud let his own gaze streak swiftly ahead, at the rest of the line. There wasn't a fair-skinned child in the bunch. But the captain wasn't letting himself do it that way. He was looking the children over, one at a time. He probably already knew; his child was not here. But he wasn't admitting it to himself. He was slowly, painfully working his way down this ragged line, avoiding as long as he could the admission that he was looking for something he would not find.

Cloud felt his throat tighten, and he turned away. This, then, was the torment he had seen in Aaron Barcroft.

"Miguel," he heard the captain say, "this girl doesn't look Comanche. I think she's Mexican."

Cloud faced back to see. Stark fear lay in the black eyes of a girl seven or eight years old. A squaw had a tight grip on her arm. Miguel touched the squaw's hand and spoke sharply. The squaw loosened her hold, and the girl suddenly ran forward, throwing her arms around the captain's legs. She began to sob out something in Spanish.

Barcroft leaned down and touched his hand to her hair and looked to Miguel. Miguel listened to the girl cry out her story. Finally he said, "She is captive, *Capitán*, many months. She begs for us to take her home."

"Where is her home?"

"Mexican settlement west of San Antonio. The Comanches they take her last spring."

What Cloud saw then made him shake his head in disbelief. A tear worked a thin trail down the captain's dusty cheek. Barcroft's voice went soft. "Tell her we'll get her home."

The captain didn't finish looking at the children. He seemed to know he wouldn't find what he had been searching for. He stood with his eyes closed, his hands gentle on the shoulders of the little Mexican girl.

Cloud turned and walked away, wondering how he could so misjudge a man.

Later, when the men had eaten and filled their canteens and drunk all the water they wanted, the captain said, "We'll catch fresh horses and take that herd back with us. But first, search out all these tepees. Anything that can be used for a weapon, bring it and pile it up here."

In short time there was a small pile of lances, bows and arrows. What rifles and other firearms the men found, they kept for their own use.

Miguel brought out a hide bag of poor gunpowder he had found in a tepee. He poured this over the pile. The captain said, "Is that all?" No one had anything else to add, so he said, "Burn it."

Miguel fired his pistol into the powder and set it ablaze.

As the flames licked up into the pile of weapons, the captain turned to Elkin. "Originally I had thought we'd burn all the tepees and make it a clean sweep. But with all their men dead, I suppose we can afford a little mercy for these women and children."

"Maybe it will teach them to have a little themselves," Elkin commented.

"Never," Barcroft gritted. He moved away from the fire and walked toward the arbor where Johnson had been taking care of the wounded. Hesitantly, Cloud followed after him.

"How're they doing, Johnson?" Barcroft asked.

The young medic replied, "Rough in spots, but I suppose they'll be able to travel. All except one. He just died."

Barcroft nodded grimly. Then he looked at Tommy Sides as he said, "It won't be easy, but a man can take a lot when he's riding in the direction of home."

Pale, his eyes sick with shock, the kid managed a weak smile. "Yes, sir, I'll make it."

"Sure you will. You've made a good soldier, son."

"Thank you, sir," the boy whispered.

As Barcroft turned away, Cloud said uncertainly, "Captain, I'd kind of like to have a word with you." He motioned with his chin. "Over here someplace."

The stiff reserve was still in Barcroft's eyes as he looked at Cloud. But he said, "I suppose so. Why not?"

They walked together out away from the tepees. Barcroft found a place on the green grass of the creekbank and sat down. Cloud squatted on his heels. He fumbled a little, hunting for the words.

"You see, sir, well . . . I sort of got started on the wrong foot, so to speak. I think maybe you got an apology comin'. What I mean to say is, I said some hard things. I thought some things even harder than what I said, after what happened about that squaw. I sort of got the notion you had a big chunk of lead instead of a heart . . . or somethin' like that.

"I didn't know about your wife and your little girl then. Man goes through a thing like that, he sees things different from other folks, I guess."

Barcroft didn't look at Cloud. A vague wall still stood between them. Cloud guessed it always would.

"Cloud, killing that squaw was a thing somebody had to do, and I did it. I took no pleasure in it. But I've not let it haunt me, either. What *does* haunt me is the way my wife looked when I found her. It wasn't the bucks who finally killed her. They turned her over to the squaws. It was a terrible death."

Barcroft rubbed his face, and Cloud could see the bone-weariness that had settled over the man. Barcroft said, "They're still women, and I try to avoid killing them when I can. But if I have to do it, I don't back away. When I look at a Comanche—man or woman—I can still see my wife the way she was that day."

Cloud pulled his gaze away from the captain's face. "What about the little girl? Have you ever found any trace of her?"

Barcroft shook his head. "Never a trace. The federal government had an Indian reservation in Young County then. I trailed my wife's killers back onto the reservation. The Indian agent and Yankee troops turned me back at the line. They said I was wrong, that none of their Indians had been out. I tried to slip in, to hunt for my little girl. One of those Yankees shot me.'' Hatred colored his voice as he spoke. ''A little later a bunch of the Comanches jumped the reservation and headed for the high plains to join the wild tribes. If my little girl was still alive, they had her with them.''

He paused a little, remembering. ''She's six now, if she's living. She was so little she probably wouldn't even remember anything about me, or about her mother. She probably wouldn't look the same. Maybe I wouldn't even know her.'' He clenched his fist, then let it go. ''Sure, she's probably dead. Most likely they killed her early and left her somewhere. In a way, I guess I hope they did. But I don't *know,* Cloud, that's what drives me crazy, I don't *know*. I keep thinking to myself, *maybe* she's still out there. I wake up in the middle of the night seeing her face. *Maybe* if I look long enough I'll find her.''

With his thumb and forefinger he rubbed the bridge of his nose, his eyes closed tight. ''I've got Miguel down there now, questioning those squaws. Someday perhaps we'll find someone who knows something. Someday . . .''

He broke off and looked away, down the creek.

Cloud stood up. Uncomfortable, he started to say something more, reconsidered and backed off, leaving the captain there alone.

Cloud caught the slight movement beyond a fringe of brush, far out in the grass. He didn't believe it at first. He tried to find it again, and it had disappeared. The wind, he thought, a glimpse of shadow as the grass bent aside. Then he spotted it again, just for an instant.

A squaw? A buck who had gotten away? It didn't seem reasonable. The Texans had made a good search of the whole camp.

The third time he knew it was more than a shadow, more than just the play of the wind. He caught his horse and moved out that way for a closer look. Whatever it was, it was a good three hundred yards from the village.

Tensing, he drew his six-shooter, holding it high and ready. At first, it was hard to tell where the thing had been. Then he caught it—something light brown—out there in the sun-cured grass. An animal—a dog, perhaps?

Suddenly it leaped up and began to run. A woman—a squaw with a bundle in her arms—a baby.

"How in the . . ." Cloud choked off the question and touched spurs to the horse.

Rapidly overtaking the woman, he shouted, "Stop there!" He didn't know how to say it in Comanche, but he figured she would know well enough what he meant. She kept running. He put the horse in beside her and slowed it down. "Now looky here, woman. . . ."

She jerked away from him and suddenly headed off at an angle, fleet as a deer.

"Whoa there," he shouted. "There ain't nobody goin' to hurt you." He reined after her. For an instant she looked back over her shoulder at him. That was her undoing, for she tripped and sprawled in the grass. The bundle went rolling, and Cloud heard a baby's plaintive cry.

He slid his horse to a stop and jumped down. He reached the baby before the mother could get up. He unrolled the blanket for a quick look. He carefully examined the small brown head, the arms, the legs.

"Don't seem like he's hurt none, 'cept his feelin's," he said, knowing as he spoke that the woman couldn't understand him. She dropped to her knees and examined the baby for herself. She grabbed it up then, wrapping the blanket around it and smothering its cries. She turned her blazing eyes on Cloud.

Cloud gasped. They were blue eyes!

For a moment he just stood and stared at her, struck dumb. Then he said haltingly, "Why, you're . . . you're a *white* woman!"

She drew back from him as if she understood nothing. She held the baby tighter against her breasts and looked at him with defiance flaming in her eyes.

"L-look, ma'am," Cloud stammered, "d-don't you understand? You're a white woman, like I'm a white man. You're not no Indian."

He took a step forward, and she stepped backward, her eyes wide.

Crazy woman. Cloud thought then. *That's what she must be, a crazy woman. She's forgotten about her own kind.*

"Look, lady," he tried again, "I just want to help you. Help you. Can't you understand?"

She trembled, but she held her ground. A question formed in her eyes. She tried once to speak, but nothing came. Then she said haltingly, "Help? . . . Help me?"

A long breath went out of Cloud, and he smiled thinly. "Well, you do know English after all."

"English." She studied the word a moment. "Yes, I know English."

The words came hard for her, as if she were reaching somewhere far back to find them, somewhere back in distant memory.

"How long have you been with the Comanches?" Cloud asked.

"How long? Very long. Very long."

Cloud reached out to grasp her arm, to start her toward the village. She pulled away again, frightened. Patiently he said, "Look, ma'am, I told you I ain't a-goin' to hurt you. We're goin' to take you back—back to your own people."

"People?" Again the question in her eyes. "My people? My people here."

"No, I don't mean the Indians. I mean white folks—*your* folks."

"No white people mine. I am Nocona. Nocona."

Nocona, Cloud thought. Sure, that's one of the Comanche bands. He shook his head, pitying her. He studied her face. She was so brown from the sun that she could pass for an Indian unless a person looked closely. But there were the blue eyes, and her hair was only brown—not Indian black. She did not have the typical round face one usually found in the Comanche. Hers was oval, a white woman's face. Very likely an attractive face, if it had had the chance. But a silent tale of hardship lay in her eyes, the sun-parched skin, the work-rough hands.

"Come on," he said gently, "let's go back to the village."

Plain enough that English was hard for her. He had heard it was that way with people who were in an alien land and never used their own language. With time, they lost it.

Miguel can talk to her in Comanche, he thought. *Then maybe we can find out something. Maybe she'll understand what we're going to do for her.*

"Come on," he said again. "Don't be afraid."

No one paid much attention as they first came in. Just a stray squaw Cloud had found. Then the word spread like wildfire. White woman!

Captain Barcroft came on the run. He shouldered roughly through the crowding circle of curious men. "Where is she?"

Cloud said, "This is her, Captain." He motioned toward the pitiable little figure who stood fear-stricken in the center of this group of staring men. Afraid of the other Texans, she somehow moved toward Cloud for protection.

The captain saw the fear in her eyes. He removed his hat, bowed from the waist in the old Texan style and said quietly, "You've got nothing to be worried about from now on, ma'am. You're with your own kind now." When she made no reply, Barcroft glanced at Cloud. "Who is she?"

"I don't know, sir."

"Who are you, ma'am?" the captain asked.

Hesitantly she said something in Comanche. The captain looked puzzled. Miguel Soto spoke up. "She use a Comanche name, *Capitán*. It mean Little Doe."

"But I want her *white* name, her real name."

Cloud spoke up. "Maybe she doesn't remember it, sir."

Incredulous, the captain demanded, "What do you mean she doesn't remember it? How long has she been with these Indians, anyway?"

He reached out and uncovered the baby's face. He stepped back in shock. "That's not her baby. It's an Indian baby."

Cloud said, "I reckon it's her baby, all right. She's been with these Comanches a long time."

Slowly the shock in the captain's face turned to revulsion. "My God," he breathed. "A white woman, an Indian baby. My God!" He stepped back again, shaking his head. "Why didn't they kill her when they took her? She'd have been a lot better off."

Cloud said, "She's bound to have people somewhere. They'll be glad to get her back."

"Will they?" the captain asked, bitterness in his voice. "Will they?"

The men parted to make way for him as he walked off. He strode out to the creek and stood a while looking down into its clear water. Cloud watched him, wondering what Barcroft was going to do. Then he watched the woman, watched how she tenderly rocked the baby in her arms to quiet its crying. He remembered how he had seen Mrs. Moseley doing the same.

Presently the captain came back, his head bowed. "I've decided what has to be done," he said huskily. "It's hard, but it's the only way. Miguel, she seems to know Comanche better than English. Tell her we're taking her back to her people. But tell her she'll have to leave the baby here."

Miguel hesitated. "*Capitán,* she is the mother."

Sharply Barcroft said, "I gave you an order, Miguel! Tell her!"

Miguel spoke quickly, plainly hating what he had to say. The woman cried out and clutched the baby tightly. She tried to break away, but stopped at sight of the Texans standing behind her. She broke into English. "No, no. My baby! My baby!"

Barcroft could not bring himself to look at the woman. "Cloud, take the baby and give it to one of the squaws."

Cloud stood with his fists tight, anger swelling in him. He didn't move.

Barcroft's voice lashed at him as it had at Miguel. "Doesn't anybody here understand an order?"

"She's the baby's mother," Cloud argued, his face darkening. "You don't just pull a mother away from her own child that way."

"It's for her own good, don't you see? How will she be treated when she goes back to civilization with an Indian baby in her arms? She'll be cast out like a leper."

"She might prefer that to losin' her baby. You ought to know how it is, Captain, to lose a baby."

That hurt. Cloud could see the pain of it in Barcroft's dark eyes. Some of the anger went out of the man's voice, but the resolve was still there. "Yes, I know. I know better than any man here what it's going to cost this woman. But in the end, she'll know it was for the best.

When she's back with her own, she'll forget all this. Perhaps she'll marry a good man and have more children, and she'll forget this one was ever born."

Cloud argued, "No woman ever forgets a baby."

Seeing no one else would do it, the captain stepped up to her and said, "Let me have the child."

She cried out, but he took the baby from her arms and turned away. He walked between the silent men, pausing long enough to say, "Get ready, men. We'll be riding in a minute."

A wrinkled old squaw walked forward to meet the captain. She took the baby and folded it tenderly to her bosom.

Cloud saw the woman's eyes pleading with him.

Stop him! a voice cried in Cloud. *Stop this thing now, before it's too late!*

"Ma'am," he said, "there's nothin' I can do."

She fell to her knees, sobbing in anguish, and the heart went out of him. He said it again, for his own benefit rather than hers:

"There's nothin' I can do."

Five

THE WIND HAD COOLED AND THE EDGE WAS WELL gone from the day's heat when the Rifles swung onto their horses and splashed out across the hoof-muddied creek, driving with them the whole horse band taken from the Indians. Gone was their weariness, swept away by the eruption of violence and the taste of victory.

Riding an Indian saddle, the white woman twisted sideways and looked back. On the hoof-pocked bank of the creek, the old squaw stood shoulder-slumped, the infant in her arms. Tears glistened on the white woman's cheeks. She forced herself to turn forward in the saddle again, straightening, her chin high, her face stony. There were no more tears. It was as if she saw nothing, felt nothing.

They rode a long time that way, heading south and a little east, the cooling north wind to their backs. Covertly, Cloud watched the woman, and he knew the other men were watching her too. She held herself rigidly aloof.

Whatever turmoil might have boiled within her, she gave no outward sign of it.

Captain Barcroft called no supper halt. The men had wolfed food in the Indian camp, and he figured they needed no more. It was a long way home. He wanted to put all the miles he could between them and the Comanche village before they quit for the night.

The time of the full moon had passed. Now a thin slice of moon, fragile as a pine shaving, provided the only light by the time Barcroft decided he had pushed horses and men as far as they would go. He held up his hand to halt the men in front. In the darkness, some of the riders bumped their horses against those in front of them before they knew of the halt.

"Far enough," the captain called. "Picket your horses. Elkin will assign guard duty."

Picketing was out of the question for the Indian horse band. Elkin had to set up an extra guard to take care of it. Cloud drew first guard. Before going out, he untied the blanket from behind his saddle and took it down, bending the roll over his arm. He sought out the woman. Barcroft had assigned her a place inside the circle of men to discourage her from trying to get away.

"Ma'am," Cloud said, "that old blanket you got don't look like much. Thought maybe you might like to use mine. I won't be in need of it noway."

She gave no sign that she had heard him. He tried to hand her the blanket, but she put her hands behind her back, her eyes defiantly avoiding him.

Cloud swallowed. He stood waiting uncertainly a moment, wondering if she might relent. Then he knew she wouldn't. This was how it would remain. "Sorry, ma'am. Reckon I can't blame you none." He spread out the blanket anyway and walked off, leaving it for her. He didn't look back, but he felt she was watching him.

He stood his tour of duty. It was difficult because of the near-darkness and a tendency of the horses to drift. His time done, he stretched out on the ground, leaning his head against his saddle. It was a hard, ungiving pillow, but better than the brittle grass tickling the back of his neck.

Cloud was deeply weary, his body aching and crying for rest. Yet he could not sleep. He kept thinking of the white woman he had found.

Who was she? Where had she come from?

He began trying to compare her with women he had known, and none seemed to fit. He found himself linking her with Lige Moseley's daughter, Samantha. There was much that was alike in them. Not town girls, either one. Yet both might be comely women if given the chance. The Comanche captive appeared to be older than Samantha by three or four years, but it was hard to tell. The harsh life of the nomadic Comanche would age a woman before her time. Still, there wasn't anything easy about the life of the Moseleys and their kind, either.

There was one big difference between the two. He had seen a wide-eyed innocence in Samantha Moseley. He knew he need not expect it in this woman. Kids grew up in a hurry around the Indian camps, for privacy was unknown, and initiation into adult life came early.

This line of thought brought him around to what worried him most—the baby. Sure, she had probably been taken by the Indians when she was too young to know much about white men's ways, white men's rules. And she was probably married, too, insofar as Indians could be married in the view of the white man. A man couldn't blame her for what had happened. Even a grown woman, taken in captivity, could not help herself.

Well, he told himself, it wouldn't happen anymore. He had found her, and she was safe now.

Safe—but at what a price!

Listening in the night, he thought once he heard her sobbing. But he finally figured out it was young Tommy Sides, tossing in fevered sleep. The woman was through sobbing now. She had that much Indian training. They would probably never hear her sobbing again.

The first flash of dawn came, and someone called for the captain. Stirring, Cloud heard a quick rise of excited talk. He arose stiffly from his bed on the grass to see what the trouble was. Sleep still clung stubbornly to him, for he had taken a long time to drop off.

"Beats me how she slipped away," he heard someone say. "I was sleepin' no more than six feet from her, and I never heard nothin'."

The captain was speaking angrily. "Someone must have heard her. She couldn't just slip out and not stir up somebody."

"She's an Indian, Captain," someone replied.

"She's white!" the captain declared emphatically. "Don't you ever forget she's a white woman!"

Calmly, Elkin said, "The men were all dog tired, Captain. Once they went to sleep, wild horses couldn't have stirred them out. I imagine you were just as tired yourself."

Barcroft cooled a little, his face twisting wryly as he caught Elkin's subtle suggestion. Elkin added, "Might be we just ought to let her go, Captain. We all know she won't be happy with her baby stayin' back yonder."

Evenly Barcroft said, "A white woman has no place in an Indian camp. And she has no place with an Indian baby in her arms. Cloud, Miguel, I want you two."

Cloud sensed the mission, and he felt a sharp regret. He wanted to say, *If that's what she wants, let's just let her go.* But he said, "What'll it be, Captain?"

Barcroft's dark eyes were sharp. "You know she's gone?"

"Figured that from the conversation."

"I want you and Miguel to go find her. She seems to have left afoot. Take her horse and bring her back."

"What if we can't find her?"

"Out on this prairie? You can find her if you want to. If you don't find her, I'll charge you with dereliction of duty. Now get yourselves a little breakfast and start out. We'll move on at an easy pace. You should be able to overtake her and then catch us."

Cloud started to turn away, then stopped. "Captain," he said thoughtfully, "I was the one found her, and I thought I was doin' her a favor. But she must've wanted to go back awful bad. And after all, we don't own her. Maybe we ought to let her do what she wants to."

Sternly Barcroft said, "Find her, Cloud!"

In that thick carpet of dry grass, it was hard to see an individual track. But most of the time, by taking a sweeping look across the prairie ahead of him, Cloud could make out the faint trace—an elusive pattern of shadow where the grass had bent down and had not come all the way up.

"Path's like an arrow, Miguel," Cloud said. "She must've took a sight on a star and followed it."

"She go straight to camp," Miguel observed, pointing. "She don' need no compass."

"That baby's compass enough. A mother that way, she's got an instinct."

The sun came up and started its long rise, heating the wind. This was going to be a scorcher of a day, thought Cloud, wiping his forehead on his sleeve. The climbing sun made the trail harder to follow, for the shadow pattern was less pronounced as sunshine spilled more directly into the bent-over grass. At times the two lost it completely. But they knew the direction and kept going. After a while they would come across a trace of the trail again.

"If she'd walked, we'd've caught her by now," Cloud said. "She must've trotted along, half-runnin' most of the time. Pushin' hard."

"She know when sunup come, we come too. She know she got to hurry. Else she don' get to camp before we catch her."

"Rate she's goin', she'll kill herself in the heat."

Gravely Miguel shrugged. "Maybeso that would be the best way. *Quién sabe,* she maybe want it like that, to kill herself."

"Don't say that, Miguel, don't say it."

Cloud tried to put the idea out of his head, but he couldn't. *She might,* he thought, *she just might. And it'll be on my shoulders, because I was the one found her.*

Then another idea came to him, and he straightened. A wild idea it was, but it might work—just *might.* "Miguel," he said, "we *could* let her go. We could tell the captain that when we caught up to her, and she saw we was fixin' to take her back, she killed herself with a knife."

Miguel pursed his lips, considering the idea. "Not bad, my frien', only where she get the knife?"

"She could've stole it from somebody as she left camp. There wouldn't be nobody own up to it noway. The captain would believe us, I reckon, if we was good enough liars."

Miguel shook his head. "You ever try to tell the *capitán* a lie?" Then he answered his own question. "No, you don't. Is not easy to look him in the eyes and say what is not true. But I let *you* tell him. Me, I don't say nothing."

Cloud still wasn't sure of himself. "Trouble is, I can't

help feelin' like maybe the captain's part right. She *is* white. She's got no business in a heathen camp thataway. If it wasn't for that baby . . ." He frowned. "Miguel, you reckon a white woman really could love a baby, knowin' its daddy was an Indian—love it, I mean, like she would if it was white? Her own kind?"

Miguel was a while in answering. "My frien', in Mexico many times the parents, they say who get married. The boy, the girl, sometimes they don' know each other, don' love each other. Maybeso they both love somebody else, and they don' even want each other. But bye and bye comes the baby, and they both love it.

"With the Indians, most time a woman she is sold for wife. Man want her, he got plenty horses, he trades for her, just like that. She marry because she is squaw and has to do what the father say. Man, he marry because he want a woman. Maybe he don' even care which one, if she is pretty—just a woman. I bet my boots this is what happen to this woman. She have a foster father, and he sell her somebody for wife. The woman, she got no say. She is for work, and to have the babies, *no más*. Maybe she don't like the man, but she will love the baby. That is woman's way."

Cloud chewed his lip, feeling the whiskers with his teeth. "Chances are her husband is dead. If we didn't get him on the trail, we likely laid him out in the camp." A cold feeling came over him. "You reckon if we let her go back to them Indians, the same thing'll happen to her all over again?"

"Young, pretty squaw, she don' stay widow long. Another man take her."

A knot started drawing up in Cloud. "Captain's right, then. Ain't Christian of us to let her go back to that. Come on, we better pick up some or she'll outrun us plumb to that camp."

There was no place for her to hide in the open, rolling prairie. When they first sighted her, she was looking back over her shoulder. She must have seen them first. Already moving at a trot, she broke into a run. Cloud and Miguel touched spurs to their horses. She ran as fast as she could. She fell once, pushed onto her feet and ran again.

They came up even with her, and Cloud swung to the ground, dropping the reins. He grabbed at her. She eluded him, only to stumble and fall. She rolled over onto her side and came up onto her knees. Sun flashed on the bright blade of a knife in her hand. Getting to her feet, her eyes stabbing in anger, she desperately brandished the blade at Cloud. He parried with his hand, drawing a thrust. He grabbed her arm and twisted it sharply. She gave a quick cry of pain and dropped the knife. Still holding her wrist, Cloud reached down for the knife and shoved it into his belt.

So she had *stolen one after all,* he thought.

He let go of her wrist then. ''I didn't go to hurt you, ma'am. You made me do it.''

She dropped to her knees, gasping for breath, and Cloud saw how thoroughly worn out she was, how she had been running. Defeat lay heavy in her eyes, but she wasn't crying. She just knelt there, her back and shoulders heaving up and down as her lungs fought for air.

Cloud took off his hat and held it in both hands. ''You made an awful good try,'' he said with admiration. ''Too bad we can't just let you go.''

She didn't try to answer him until she had her breath. Then she turned her face up to him, her blue eyes pleading. ''Please, please, that is my home.'' She spoke slowly, the words still difficult for her. ''My baby is there. Why can't I go? You took no other woman.''

''You're a white woman, the only one there was.''

''I am not white woman. My face is white, my eyes

are the eyes of a white woman. I have often been ashamed of that. But my heart is Nocona. My baby is Nocona. Why do you want me?''

Cloud looked to Miguel for help and got none. ''But you *are* white,'' he said, knowing it wasn't answer enough. ''That's all the reason there is.'' Now it was Cloud who pleaded with his eyes, pleaded for her to understand. ''Ma'am, you grew up with the Indians, so there's a lot you can't know. There's things a white woman just don't do. You get back to the settlements, and live awhile with your own folks, you'll understand what I'm tryin' to tell you.''

Despair colored her voice. ''I don't want to go to the white people. I want to go to my baby. It is a weak baby, a sick baby. It needs me.''

For a moment Cloud thought she would cry. His throat tightened in sympathy for her. Again he looked to Miguel and got no help.

''Miguel,'' he said, ''ain't there nothin' you can say to her?''

Miguel shook his head, and Cloud could see in the Mexican's eyes a dislike for the task they had to do. ''There is nothing to say. We follow the order, like it or not. The *capitán* say she come, she come.''

Cloud looked at the bereaved woman and wished he had never seen her. He turned away, flexing his hands.

There *was* a way, he thought suddenly.

He turned back. ''Miguel, how far you reckon it is to that Indian camp?''

Miguel shrugged. ''She come pretty far. Two, maybeso three more miles.''

To the woman Cloud said, ''What if we went with you into that camp to get your baby? Would you come out with us again, and no fuss?''

The woman looked up quickly, sudden hope in her face. "You would let me get my baby?"

Miguel pointed out in argument, "The *capitán,* he don' like it."

"I don't care. It just ain't natural to take this woman away from her baby, no matter what color it is."

"He raise plenty hell with us."

"But he can't turn back anymore, and he can't just leave the baby out on the prairie."

Miguel shrugged. Cloud could tell he wasn't keen about the idea. "Whatever you say, my frien', I go with you. But we have to watch those squaws. They get the chance, they cut us to pieces."

"We'll watch." To the woman he said, "How about it? Promise to come out with us again and not give us no trouble?"

Tears of joy shone in her eyes. "I promise. I promise."

He reached down and took her hands and helped her to her feet. The warmth of her hands stirred him, and for a moment he held them. She pulled the hands away, letting her blue eyes briefly meet his with their glow of gratitude. "You have good heart, *Tejano.*"

"I got a conscience," he told her, "and for a little while there, it didn't like me much."

He helped her onto her horse, and they headed toward the village. Miguel moved out a little in the lead, watching ahead of them nervously. Worry rode heavy on the Mexican's shoulders.

Cloud tried to watch the prairie too, but most of the time he watched the woman. He watched the graceful way she sat the Comanche saddle, her back straight, her shoulders square. She would glance at him and catch him looking at her, and she would look away again.

"You know somethin', ma'am?" he found himself telling her. "Get you back to civilization, put some good clothes on you and do your hair up settlement-style, you're goin' to look pretty—right pretty." He felt a flush of embarrassment then and wished he hadn't said it. But she didn't seem to have understood. He could see the eagerness in her eyes, and he knew she was thinking only of the baby.

He rode a while farther before he finally asked her, "What's your name, ma'am? Your white name, I mean."

She shook her head. "My white name? Easter. Easter Rutledge." A look of wonder came into her face. "It has been a long time since I have said that name. Easter Rutledge. Easter Rutledge." She spoke the name slowly, almost as if she were carefully tasting something that had a strange new flavor. "It sounds . . . I don't know what to say . . . funny. It is like the name of someone else."

"Don't reckon you've had much chance to use it. How long you been with the Comanches?"

"Long ago they took me—many, many years ago. I was a little girl. I do not remember much—the shooting, the screams. My white father—I am sure he died. My mother . . . I can't remember. It has been so long ago." She looked down, frowning, trying to recall the far-distant past. "I was given a new father and mother in the Noconas. With them I was not white. I was Nocona. Always I have been Nocona."

Cloud observed, "You're gettin' better with your English. You must've had some practice on it."

"There was a white woman with us many years. Slave. Always she called me Easter. Always she spoke English. She said I must never forget my English, must never forget I was white. I told her I was not white—I was Nocona. But I spoke English with her. She died two or three winters ago. Since then I have not spoken with a white person. I have not spoken English."

Cloud was a little hesitant about the next question, and

he waited awhile before he asked it. "You have a husband?"

She shook her head. "He is dead."

"Was he . . . I mean, did you love him?"

"Love?" She seemed a little puzzled by the word. "He brought me food. He gave me my son."

"But were you in love with him?"

She frowned. "I don't know what you mean."

Cloud nodded, satisfied. "You weren't, I reckon, or you'd *know* what I meant." The thought made him feel better, somehow.

They rode awhile in silence, following Miguel. They were into the rolling hills now, not far from the creek where the camp stood.

"Soon now," Cloud heard the woman speaking softly, more to herself than to him. "Soon now." Her face was happy.

Easing up a rise, Miguel Soto suddenly stopped. The way he stiffened in the saddle, Cloud knew something was wrong. Miguel held up his hand in a signal for the other two to halt. Cloud did, for a moment, then he and Easter Rutledge moved slowly forward, drawing abreast of Miguel.

Somberly Miguel turned to her and said, "Very bad luck, señora. Very bad luck."

He pointed. Cloud could see the riders down yonder, strung out in a dusty line along the creek, pushing a small bunch of horses straight toward the ravaged camp.

"Comanches," Cloud breathed. "Another raidin' party just comin' in. And way too big for us."

He turned regretfully to the woman, to tell her what this meant. He saw despair drive the glow from her face.

He didn't have to tell her. She already knew.

Six

BRUSH HILL WAS NOT MUCH OF A TOWN, EVEN AS frontier settlements went. It had been built with little view toward permanence and no view at all toward beauty. Money scarce the way it was, few people could afford to buy much in the form of niceties or comforts. Either they built what they wanted out of what was at hand, or they did without.

Besides, there were the Comanches to worry about. No use in a man spending months of labor and breaking his heart building something the Indians might burn down in minutes. Main thing at first was to put up something with a roof on it to keep the family in the dry, and something that would provide a man a solid wall to stand behind with his guns in case the Indians came. There would be a time later to build the fine homes the womenfolks dreamed of, a time when there was money in circulation and no longer any need to worry about "John" sneaking in on a moonlit night to put it all to the torch.

Cloud had seen a lot of settlements like Brush Hill, although he had not been in this one before. It was a loose scattering of picket and log houses, for the most part, each having its garden and shed and outbuildings, its cedar-stake corral to hold the stock. Oldest house—by the aging of its logs Cloud figured it to have been up six or eight years—was built next to a spring which percolated out of a rock outcrop and formed a deep, clear pool. From the pool flowed a small creek, winding its erratic way down through the grassy hills, seeking a level spot it wouldn't find.

The newer the houses, the farther down the creek they sat.

Approaching the settlement, Cloud had seen the plowed fields, the crops mostly burned now under the barren heat of the summer sun, the moisture-robbing search of the dry wind which moaned down from the high plains. He had seen the settlers' cattle, scattered over a hundred hills and more.

Here lay a land of promise, a fresh new land which had seen far more of the Indian than of the white man, far more of the buffalo than of the new spotted cattle, a land which for the most part had still not felt the rip of the plow. Small wonder, thought Cloud, the Indians hated to see it go.

But he felt, as most settlers did, that the Indians had no solid claim upon it. They had come only now and again in search of game, touching lightly like the wind, leaving no mark upon the land, neither building nor tearing down.

Judging from the widely scattered houses he had seen, Cloud would estimate there were fifteen or twenty families in Brush Hill settlement. He saw one large log building he took to be a store. There wasn't much a frontier store could handle except the barest essentials of life, for its customers had a hard enough time buying even those. Here a man earned his daily bread by raising the stuff that went into it. If he didn't raise it, he didn't eat.

Mighty little room in a settlement like this for the riff-raff that so often gravitated to the land beyond the law. To make a living here they would have to work for it. Plain to see there wasn't any loose money floating around.

Cloud wouldn't have expected the Rifles to attract much of a crowd here, because there just weren't that many people. But it seemed everybody was out to watch the men bringing in that big string of recovered horses. Children ran and shouted, and chased afoot after the horsemen. Men grinned as they recognized mounts they had lost.

"Hey, Elkin," someone shouted, "did you get back that blue roan of mine?"

Elkin called to him, "We're fixin' to pen them down at the camp. Come along and look them over."

As the horses passed, eyes of the watchers touched first upon the little Mexican girl riding alongside Miguel Soto. Then, inevitably, they would find the buckskin-clad woman of the brown hair and the blue eyes, riding beside the dark-bearded man named Cloud. Cloud could see people pointing to her. Though he couldn't hear them, he knew they were talking about her. And by the way she rode with her chin down, her eyes half closed, he knew she knew it.

White woman, the word raced down the road. *They've rescued a white woman.*

They passed by the store, and Cloud could see the aproned proprietor with three or four other men, standing on the narrow front porch. Atop a low, slender flagpole flew the Texas flag. Cloud stared at it.

The red-haired Quade Guffey said, "They used to fly the United States flag, but come secession they hauled her down. Ain't nobody out here got a Confederate flag, so they use the old Lone Star in its place."

Captain Barcroft had been riding up at the head of the column, out of the dust. Now he dropped back, holding still while the horse herd moved past him. When the last of them had gone by, he cut in behind and signaled Cloud to stop.

His glance went to the woman, then just as quickly left her. Cloud had seen Barcroft look at her this way many times since he and Miguel had brought her back to the command. There was an uneasiness in his manner with the woman, almost a distaste. The captain had avoided any unnecessary conversation with her, except that he had asked her once if she had seen a little white girl with the Indians. She told him she hadn't.

Since then, the captain seemed to have gone out of his way to stay away from her. Yet he often glanced at her, as if in the grip of some fascination he wanted to avoid.

"Cloud," he said, "Miguel will take the girl to a Mexican family at the edge of the settlement. I thought we might bring Missus . . . Miss Rutledge here to these people at the store. I think the Lawtons will take care of her until we can find out more about her and get in touch with her own people."

Without exactly saying so, Barcroft seemed to have delegated Cloud to be Easter Rutledge's guardian. When the captain was around, she would stand steadfast and stare straight ahead, as if she could not see or hear him. But she somehow seemed to accept Cloud, to look upon him as something of a buffer against the tall, dark-eyed officer with the grim voice, the unsmiling face.

Maybe he looks on both of us as outcasts, Cloud thought. *Figures we make a pair.*

Easter Rutledge had not talked since their failure to get into the Indian camp, except to say the things that had to be said. She had not offered to tell any more of her past, and Cloud had not tried to question her. As he saw it, when she felt like talking, she would. You couldn't expect much from a woman who had just been forced to give up her baby.

The captain rode past the front of the store. The proprietor, heavyish and balding, with an old man's step, moved off the porch. "Welcome back, Aaron," he spoke to the captain, a genuine gladness in his voice. But his eyes were on Easter Rutledge.

"Thank you, Mister Lawton," the captain responded. "Is Mother Lawton at home?"

"Just go on back," Lawton said.

The Lawton house behind the store was a double cabin, somewhat like Lige Moseley's had been, with a dog run in the center and an extra lean-to on one side. A young woman stood on the dog run, watching the three riders approach, the old proprietor following along afoot. As Barcroft stepped down and dropped his reins over the cedar-stake fence, she hurried out to meet him. He moved through the gate and stopped.

"Hello, Hanna," he said.

She reached out as if to put her arms around him, reconsidered and drew her hands back against her body. "Aaron," she said softly, a catch in her voice. She summoned up strength and said, "Aaron, it's good to see you back. We were worried."

She was tall and slender, a strongly handsome woman in her early twenties. At first Cloud thought she could be Barcroft's sister, but he decided against it when the captain said, "We came to see your mother."

Still at a loss as to what she should do with her hands, the young woman finally crossed her arms. Cloud thought he could see a trace of tears in her eyes. Tears of relief, he thought. "She's in the house," she said. "I'll call her." She walked back toward the cabin and called, "Mother, Aaron's home."

An elderly woman stepped out through the open cabin door onto the dog run, her hands wrapped in an apron, her eyes wide in joy. "Aaron! You're all right? Not hurt or anything?"

"Just fine," he told her. She walked to him, gripped his arm and pulled him down to kiss him on the cheek. For a moment the captain seemed to soften. Then he glanced at Cloud and Easter Rutledge, still sitting on their horses outside the yard fence. He regained his stiff composure. "Mother Lawton," he said, "I've brought someone who is going to need help."

For the first time the two women in the yard noticed Easter Rutledge. There was a moment of shocked silence as they looked her over, taking in the buckskin clothes, the fringed mocassins, the Comanche braids in her long brown hair.

Then the older woman stepped to the gate, lifting her hands as if to help Easter down. "You poor child," she said with concern, "you must be completely worn out. Come on in with us."

Cloud swung down from his saddle and turned to help Easter. She glanced at him desperately as if asking him what to do.

"It's all right, Easter," he told her, not even conscious of speaking her first name instead of the "ma'am" he had used so much. "These folks are goin' to help you."

Mother Lawton's gray eyes were wide with anxiety as she looked the girl over again. "Those clothes! Land sakes, you've been held by those Indians, haven't you? You poor child!" She bit her lower lip in an unconscious gesture of sympathy. "I'll bet you're glad to be back among Christian folk again. It's God's blessing that our Aaron found you."

Easter Rutledge looked at the ground. Her shoulder jerked in the beginning of a sob before she could catch herself. Mother Lawton put her hands on the girl's shoulders and spoke gently, "There now, there's no need to cry anymore. Everything's fine now, just fine."

Captain Barcroft said quietly, "Before it goes any farther, Mother Lawton, there's something you should know. She's lived among the Indians so long she doesn't feel she's really white. We brought her against her will."

The gray-haired woman looked up sharply. "Against her will? I don't believe it." Her gaze dropped to the girl again. She shook her head slowly. "Then she's more to be pitied than ever. Only god knows how many kidnapped girls there are out yonder like this one, slaves to the heathen."

She took Easter's chin in her hand and looked into the young woman's glistening eyes. "You won't be unhappy long, child. You'll get used to the ways of your own again, and you'll be able to live as a Christian. You'll be glad you came back."

Still Easter did not speak. Barcroft said, "One more thing. You'll learn it soon enough, so I'll tell you now. She had an Indian husband. And she had a baby—an Indian baby."

The old woman's eyes went wide again. "A baby?" She paused, absorbing the idea and finally accepting it. "Well, where is it?"

"We left it behind," said Barcroft.

"You *left* it?" The sharp rise of her voice seemed to surprise Barcroft a little.

"We thought . . . *I* thought it best not to bring it. It'll be hard enough for this woman to readjust herself to white people's ways without having a half-Indian child along. You know the stigma it would attach to her."

Easter dropped her chin again. She closed her eyes, but

not before a tear squeezed out and ran down her cheek.

The old woman stood in silence, the anger rising in her face. Then she blazed, "Aaron Barcroft, sometimes you're the smartest man I know, and sometimes you're a fool. This time you're a fool!"

The younger woman named Hanna spoke up in protest. "Mother . . ."

Anger came into Barcroft's face. "I thought it would be better for her in the long run. I still do."

"And you're still a fool!"

Hanna Lawton stepped quickly to Aaron Barcroft. "Aaron," she said, "Mother's sorry. She says things she doesn't mean."

"She means it, all right," Barcroft replied tightly. "But when she thinks about it some, she'll know I'm right. It was the only way, the only right and proper way."

Mrs. Lawton paid little attention. Her arm around Easter's shoulder, she guided the girl toward the cabin. "Come on into the house, child. Come on in with me."

Hanna Lawton stood by the captain and watched her mother take Easter inside. Her fingertips were white as she unconsciously dug them into her crossed arms. Her eyes were plainly sympathtic to Easter, but she seemed hesitant to say anything that might hurt Barcroft. "It's going to be hard for her, Aaron. Perhaps you don't know what a sacrifice you've forced her to make."

Pain tightened the captain's face. "Hanna, you—above all people—ought to realize what I know about sacrifice."

She reached out and touched his arm, then pulled her hand away. "Yes, Aaron. I'm sorry—I shouldn't have said it. Sometimes a man has to do what he thinks is right, no matter how hard it may be."

Barcroft left the yard, turning back a moment at the gate. "I'll be back tonight, Hanna, when I've had a chance to clean up some. By then your mother may feel more like talking to me.''

''Please do that, Aaron.''

As he swung into the saddle and started away, she said again, ''It's good to have you back.''

Barcroft glanced then at Cloud, as if he had forgotten him. ''Never did introduce you, did I?'' it occurred to him. He studied a moment and said, ''You'll come back with me later. That girl seems to have decided she can trust you. Maybe you can get her to tell us where her home is.''

Cloud nodded, glad somehow that he hadn't seen the last of Easter Rutledge. ''I'll try, sir.''

Riding away, he glanced over his shoulder. Hanna Lawton still stood in the yard, watching them. Cloud said, ''You've known these folks a long time, Captain?''

''A long time, Cloud. A long, long time.'' Barcroft's face was grave. He seemed to reach far back into memory a little while, then he said, ''My wife was a Lawton. The old folks there, they were her mother and father.''

''Then the one you called Hanna . . .''

Barcroft nodded again. ''Hanna was her sister.''

The store was closed and dark when they rode back in the dusk. At the cabin in the rear, a lantern glowed on the narrow porch, showing the way to the door. Cloud and Barcroft swung down from their horses and dropped their reins over the stake fence. Cloud stepped to the gate first and held it open for the captain. He rubbed his clean-shaven chin.

''Miss Rutledge may not know us now, sir,'' he commented. ''Bath in the creek, clean clothes and a shave—I don't hardly know myself.''

The captain never even attempted a reply as he walked through the gate.

Hanna Lawton had heard the horses. She stepped out onto the porch, into the yellow glow of the lantern. As the captain moved up to her, she held out her hand. He gripped it a moment.

"We've been expecting you, Aaron."

"How's your mother?"

"She has her temper under control. But she hasn't changed her mind."

"I'll not argue with her," the captain said. "Nobody can."

Hanna Lawton's gaze rested on Cloud, and curiosity was in her eyes. Barcroft said, "Hanna, this is Sam Houston Cloud. He's a new recruit in the Rifles. I've put him up as scout with Miguel Soto. It was Cloud who found the white woman."

Hat in his hand, Cloud bowed from the waist. "Ma'am."

Hanna Lawton said, "It's a pleasure to meet you, Mister Cloud." It wasn't just something she said because it was customary. Cloud got the feeling she honestly meant it. In this sparsely settled country, strangers didn't remain strangers long. Frontier dwellers lost the veneer of cool reserve that people so often held to in heavily settled country. A new face was always welcome, unless it brought trouble.

Cloud asked her, "How's she feelin'—Miss Rutledge, I mean? She makin' out all right?"

Hanna Lawton shook her head. "It's hard to tell. She's a little bewildered yet. And sad, too. She won't say so, but she's thinking about"—she glanced quickly at the captain—"about her baby."

The captain asked, "Has she told you anything about her home—where the Comanches stole her from?"

"Nothing, Aaron. But we haven't pushed her. We thought it best to try to make her feel as much at ease as we could, not upset her with a lot of questions.'

"Well," said Barcroft, "the questions will have to be asked, sooner or later, if we're to get her back to her home. May we go in?"

"Surely, Aaron. I didn't mean to keep you standing around outside."

She motioned toward the open door. Cloud and the captain stepped up onto the rough-hewn porch. Cloud stamped his boots to get the dust off. He had an idea from the looks of the outside that this cabin would have a plank floor, and he wouldn't want to get it dirty. Barcroft went in first, as befitted an officer. Cloud trailed, pausing to motion for Hanna Lawton to go in ahead of him.

He saw Easter Rutledge then, and the sight of her brought a quick stab of surprise.

The Indian clothes were gone. Although her face was burned a deep brown by the sun, she was unmistakably white in a rather plain sort of homespun cotton dress that fitted tightly around her slim waist and flowed full to the floor. The braids had been taken from her brown hair, the hair washed and rolled up into a round bun at the back of her neck. A simple white ribbon had been tied around the bun.

"By Ned!" Cloud breathed, "I don't believe it!"

Protest formed in the captain's eyes. He turned to Hanna Lawton. "That dress—is it—"

She said quickly, "It's one of mine."

Barcroft nodded then, relieved. "I thought for a minute . . ."

Mother Lawton stood beside the girl, proudly looking over the changes she had been able to accomplish since afternoon. "Aaron," the old lady said, "you still have all of Celia's things packed away in that big leather-bound trunk. They'll do no one any good there. This girl could certainly use some of them. Why don't you—"

"No," the captain spoke sharply. "They were *hers*! I'll give them to no—" He broke off, for he had said more than he intended to. The quick anger settled, but a trace of it remained in the hard set of his mouth. "We'll leave her clothes in that trunk!"

Mother Lawton turned away, face tight. "Anything you say, Aaron."

After an uncomfortable moment, the captain introduced Cloud to the Lawtons. To old Henry Lawton, puffing calmly on his pipe, Barcroft said, "I noticed Cloud looking at your Texas flag on the store. I think he had rather it was still the Union flag."

Cloud flinched. *That was sure putting it out in the open.*

Barcroft said matter-of-factly, "He's not the only one in my command who still fancies the Union more than the Confederacy."

He's not ever going to forget that, Cloud thought darkly.

He could tell by the Lawtons' faces that they disagreed with his politics. But after a moment Mrs. Lawton said, "Well, at least Mister Cloud didn't shirk his call to duty. He joined the Rifles. There are others in this section who see things the way he does." She smiled then to set him at ease.

Henry Lawton drew thoughtfully on his pipe, eyes narrowed as he stared at Cloud. "You a native of Texas, Cloud?" When Cloud nodded, the old man reached out and shook his hand. "That's all right, then. Long's a man keeps his rifle pointed at the Indians instead of at us, I'm inclined to let his politics alone."

Cloud felt better. He knew he could get along fine with these folks.

Barcroft nodded toward Easter Rutledge and abruptly changed the subject. "We came to see what this woman can tell us about her people. We need to find out where she's from so we can return her there and get her off of our hands.'' He turned to Easter Rutledge. ''How about it?'' he asked her brusquely. ''Where was your home?''

Her eyes stabbed at him, then she turned away to stare sullenly at the cabin wall. She did not reply.

Stiffly the captain said, ''It's not for *my* benefit I'm asking you this. It's for *yours*.''

She was silent a moment. Then, not looking at him, she spoke with an edge of hatred in her voice. ''I do not talk with you, Captain. I will talk to the other man''—she pointed her chin toward Cloud—''but I do not talk to you.''

Barcroft's face darkened. He rocked back hesitantly, unaccustomed to being spoken to this way. He started to say something but bit it off short.

Henry Lawton said, ''Aaron, maybe it'd be better if you left. Let Cloud talk to her.''

Barcroft spoke tightly, ''Are you running me off, Mister Lawton?''

Mother Lawton said, ''Nobody's running you off, Aaron. But under the circumstances, it just looks as if you might better leave.''

Barcroft backed toward the door. ''As you wish, then.'' He glanced at Cloud. ''Take over, Cloud. I'm going back to camp. He paused a moment, and it appeared he was more hurt than angry. ''Good night, Mister Lawton, Missus Lawton. Good night, Hanna.''

Hanna said, ''I'll walk out with you, Aaron.''

Cloud stood first on one foot, then on the other, feeling that he was caught in the middle. When the captain had gone, he said to the Lawtons, ''He don't seem to realize how hard he's treatin' Miss Rutledge. Got a blind spot toward her, seems like.''

Mrs. Lawton looked toward the open door through

which Hanna had followed Barcroft. "Not the only blind spot he has," she said pensively.

Easter Rutledge still stared at the wall. Wanting to put her at ease, Cloud said, "Why don't you sit down, Easter . . . Miss Rutledge?" He pulled out a chair for her. She sat, but her blue eyes were still grave.

Cloud tried to appear cheerful. "Well, now, these folks have sure fixed you up pretty. I told you you'd look mighty good wearin' a white-woman dress, your hair all done up nice. You do now, and that's a fact."

Henry Lawton said, "Been a steady stream of people to the store, hopin' to catch a look at her."

Mrs. Lawton nodded. "But we've kept her pretty much out of sight. No use gettin' her all nervous with a lot of people starin' at her."

Easter had shown no response, and Cloud turned back to the Lawtons. "Sure good of you folks to take her in this way."

Mrs. Lawton shrugged away the compliment. "We're puttin' her over in the other side of the cabin, in the room with Hanna. She's welcome to stay just as long as she wants to."

"You hear that, Easter?" Cloud asked the girl. "You're goin' to like it when you get used to white people's ways. These are good folks. And they'll take real good care of you."

Easter looked at him a moment, her eyes softening. Then she said, "But there is always the captain."

"The captain, he's been through a lot, Easter. He don't really mean to be hard. He just doesn't think, sometimes."

She said firmly, "He is a bad man."

Mother Lawton sat down beside the girl and put a wrinkled hand on her arm. "Not a *bad* man, honey, a *driven* man." Easter looked blankly at her, not comprehending. Mrs. Lawton said, "Never mind, you'll understand bye and bye. Right now this young man has come to talk with you, to try to find out some things so he can help you."

Easter Rutledge dropped her chin. "Help me?" She slowly shook her head. "There is only one way to help me—get me back my baby. I tell you, it is a sick baby. It needs me. It has always been a weak baby. The women, they say it is the white blood. Without me it may die!"

Cloud swallowed. "It's too late for you to go back now. Look, ma'am, you've likely got folks someplace, white folks. We'd like to find them for you."

Her lips were tight. "My people are to the north. The Noconas are my people."

Rubbing the back of his neck, Cloud looked around helplessly at the Lawtons. Scouting Indians was something he could handle. Trying to talk soft words to a heartbroken woman was out of his realm.

Mrs. Lawton gently took the girl's hand. "Easter, he means well for you. We all do. You don't belong out there where you were. You belong in Christian company, with your own family."

Bleakly the girl said, "I belong with my baby."

Mrs. Lawton's voice was soft and kind. "God forgive him, that was a bad mistake on Aaron's part. But there's no way we can correct it now. We'll just have to go ahead and do the best we can to make things up to you, to help you. Won't you help *us*?"

For a long moment Easter Rutledge didn't answer. Finally she said, "You are good people. And you"—she looked at Cloud—"you tried to help me." She bit her lip. "I have lost all that mattered to me. I have nothing more to lose. I will tell you everything I remember. . . ."

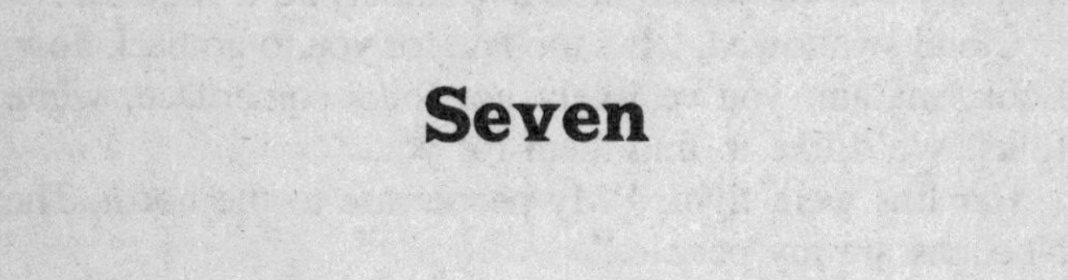

Seven

IT DIDN'T TAKE CLOUD LONG TO FIND OUT THAT SOLdiering was about one part action to ten parts routine—even frontier soldiering.

Headquarters was a heavy log house a mile or so downcreek from the store. The man who had built this house had put it up large and sturdy, a small fort atop a brush-cleared rise where Indians would have a hard time sneaking up unseen and where they'd have a harder time breaching the bull-stout walls. Bullet holes and splintered wood, darkened now with age, showed they'd tried it more than once. But eventually they'd caught the settler far out from his fortress and had left him to die in the open grass, his knife-carved body bleeding in the sun.

Now the long-abandoned house served as command post for Captain Aaron Barcroft and his company of the Texas Mounted Rifles. Rebuilt corrals held the horses, when they weren't in use or weren't being loose-herded on the prairie. Dust-grayed tents were staked in straight rows on either side of the log house, their canvas sides rolled up to let the summer heat escape, as much as it could.

On the hot days, Cloud wished the settler had left some trees for shade in which to pitch the tents. But the man had traded the shade for a better chance to keep his life.

A pole stood in front of the building, the tamped earth still fresh around its base. It was short for a flagpole, but tall trees weren't to be found in this country. Besides, the company didn't have a Confederate flag yet anyway. It had the pole, just in case a flag ever came.

A flat area below the house served as a drill ground. Here Barcroft regularly brought his well-thumbed copies of Hardee's *Light Infantry Tactics* and the U.S. Army's *Cavalry Tactics* to put the men through instruction and drill. Actually, he didn't really need the books anymore. He'd learned them by heart. Because he'd never been a soldier before—much less an officer—he'd studied hard to learn the things he needed to know. What Aaron Barcroft learned, he never forgot.

Part of company routine was to keep up a picket system along the frontier, one link in the state's chain of posts which extended all the way from the northern extremity on the Red River to the southern line on the Rio Grande. At regular intervals Barcroft dispatched men to work out in either direction, meeting riders from other companies and joining the chain. As they rode, these riders watched closely for Indian signs. Any time the Indians made a raid, they had to cross the patrol lines ridden regularly by the Texas Mounted Rifles.

The Rifles also watched for signs of white men moving west. Often these were war-evaders trying to escape service in the armies of the Confederacy. On the occasions when the Rifle patrols met such men, there was usually little they could do about them. These service-evaders usually traveled in parties big enough to stand off the Indians—or the Rifles.

Anyway, Indians were the main reason the Rifles were organized. The "scalawags" had to be put up with, like an incurable disease. Long as they didn't bother anything, the patrols usually left them alone.

Cloud found that Barcroft had a simple but effective method of getting rid of the occasional laggard or coward who found his way into the command. He worked the man's tail off or put him in the most hazardous duty. Usually it wouldn't be long before the man turned up missing on morning roll call. Though he was supposed to, the captain never sent a patrol after such a deserter to bring him back. He was afraid he might have to put up with the man again.

As to antisecessionists like Cloud, Barcroft had no clear-cut policy, other than to keep them busy. Occasionally some little animosity flared between Unionist and staunch Confederate, but most of the men kept their politics to themselves. They agreed it was more worthwhile to fight Indians than to fight each other.

An exception was a ruddy-faced, belligerent farmer named Seward Prince, who stood up for the Confederacy proud and loud, and was constantly daring any "black Republican" to say him nay. He had whipped just about every Unionist in the company, including Quade Guffey, and he kept challenging Cloud. Finally Cloud got a bellyful of it.

He walked with Prince down to the creek, out of sight. Here, completely alone, the two took off their shirts and wrestled and slugged for the better part of an hour. They kept it up until both men could hardly move. The only thing they settled was that one was about as tough as the other.

From then on, respecting one another but with no friendship between them, Cloud and Prince kept their distance as best they could.

Barcroft got wind of the fight. Afterwards, he kept Cloud assigned out on patrol duty most of the time. No sooner would Cloud drag in wearily from one scouting trip than he would get orders from Barcroft to go out on another. The only consolation was that Barcroft was working Seward Prince about as hard. Whichever way he sent Cloud, he sent Prince in the opposite direction.

Often Quade Guffey was assigned with Cloud. Riding out one day into the dry country to the west, Quade commented, "Ever seem to you like the captain's got all of us picked as has any sort of Union leanin's? Keeps us bumpin' our tailbone agin a saddle all the time. Don't give us no chance to sit around camp and talk treason."

"Keep us out of trouble," Cloud commented. "Man opens his mouth wrong these days, he can get hung for it. Maybe he's doin' us a favor, keepin' us too busy to talk. Anyway, I'd rather be out on scout than in camp havin' to drill."

Quade agreed. "Drill looks to me like a heap of foolishness. Who's goin' to ride in a column of twos—or march along in step—into a battle with the Indians?"

Cloud shrugged. "Give the devil his due; Barcroft knows what he's about. You take this drill now, it teaches discipline. Most of us in this outfit never took no orders before. Somethin' comes up we don't like, we want to stop and argue about it. But you get in a fight, you got to know how to follow an order. That's what this drill is for."

If Barcroft worked and drilled his men until they dragged, he fought for them, too. Cloud and Guffey happened to be in camp, resting from a long patrol, the day an inspector came out from Austin headquarters to look things over. He was a paunchy little man with a big nose and a quarrelsome voice that started complaining as soon as he rode up in his hack. For an hour he made the rounds with Captain Barcroft, criticizing first one thing, then another.

He pointed to Cloud and Guffey and said crossly, "I see men sitting over yonder in the shade, Captain. Orders call for plenty of drill. I suggest that you should have them out at drill instead of lounging about."

"These men are fresh in from a long scout."

"Perhaps you haven't heard, Captain, but we're at war. This is no time for weakness in men. We must be strong and hard, ready to sacrifice."

Barcroft had tried hard to contain his anger, but that was too much. He pointed to the man's soft belly and gritted, "*You* haven't done without anything, that's plain to see. Time and again you politicians have promised us what we need to carry on our job here, and time and again you've turned a deaf ear to everything I've asked you for. It's all I can to do keep these men fed. Times we don't have enough powder and lead to do our job. It's been two months since these men have been paid. You stand there fat and comfortable and talk to me about being hard, about accepting sacrifice?"

The fat man sputtered. "Captain, I'll remind you who I am—"

"I know damned well who you are, and I know *what* you are! If you press me, I'll tell you what that is. And if you don't like it, I'll let you choose your own weapons!"

The inspector was backing away. "I'll have your commission! I'll tell them back in Austin!"

"You do that! Tell them for me that they're just a bunch of grasping politicians with their fingers so deep in the pie that they don't care if the whole house is afire!

Tell them that if they don't send us what we need, I'll turn my back on the Indians and lead this company to Austin! We'll do some housecleaning there, I promise you!"

The inspector didn't even wait for supper.

Cloud and Guffey tried to hold back their grins as they watched the politician's hack pull away.

Barcroft said sharply, "You two get out of my sight or I'll set you to drilling!"

Now and again, when he had the chance, Cloud would drop by to visit Easter Rutledge at the Lawton home. Indoors much of the time now, she was beginning to lose much of the dark-brown color the outdoor life had given her. Her skin appeared to soften. Some of the grief lines had faded from around her eyes. She seemed now to be prettier than he had first thought.

The first time he saw her smile was one day when she asked him about his name, Cloud.

"Cloud," she said, then repeated the name, listening to the sound of it. "Sounds like an Indian name. You're not an Indian, are you?"

She smiled then as he assured her he was not. After that, she smiled with him more and more often.

And now that he had seen her smile, he went back to visit her more and more often.

One day, freshly bathed and shaved after a long patrol, Cloud rode up to the house behind the store and tied his horse to the fence. Mother Lawton was out sweeping the yard clean. There was no grass, so the old woman took pride in keeping her yard swept bare as her floor.

"Hello, Cloud." She smiled. "I reckon you came to see me!"

He grinned back at her. "Sure I did. Who else?"

"I couldn't imagine. But you'll find her down by the

creek. Took her slate with her. She's practicin' writin'."

Cloud's eyebrows lifted. "Learnin' fast, isn't she?"

"Hanna's work. Hanna's a natural teacher. She teaches all the kids around here, and Easter's an apt pupil."

Cloud said, "I'm glad. Maybe she'll find her way easier than we thought she would." He frowned. "How's she doin', otherwise?"

Mother Lawton shrugged, leaning on her broom. "As well as could be expected, I suppose. I mean, you couldn't expect miracles, tearin' her away like that from the people she knew, from . . . But there's times she acts almost happy for a little while."

"The people around here, they've taken to her pretty good, haven't they?"

"Most of them. She was a real curiosity at first. Everybody wanted to come and look at her. They scared her some. But she got over that—sort of come to accept it, I guess. And people liked her—most people, anyway."

"Some didn't."

"Cloud, there are always a few who won't understand. They say she's a white woman, and she ought to've killed herself rather than live with the Indians that way—take one for a husband—bear his baby. One woman even told her that, to her face."

Cloud looked sharply at Mother Lawton. "Did it hurt her?"

"Didn't hurt her as much as it made her mad. And when she gets mad, she gets Indian-mad." She smiled. "That woman never has come back. Not even to the store. Just sends her husband when she needs somethin'."

Cloud nodded. "Good for Easter."

Mother Lawton took hold of the broom again. "Well, I've got work to do. Go on down to the creek. You'll find her."

Walking down toward the water, Cloud could hear children talking. When he spotted Easter, she was sitting in a rude outdoor chair in the deep shade of cottonwood trees, several youngsters gathered around her. She was showing them the letters she had made on a slate. "Is that all right?" she asked. A little girl said, "It's fine, except the bar needs to be straight on the T. Here, I'll show you."

Cloud watched silently, smiling, until the children noticed him and Easter turned around to see what they were looking at. Cloud took off his hat. "Howdy, Easter."

"Hello, Cloud." She stood up and faced him. The children waited around until they could tell their visit with Easter was over. Then the girl who had corrected Easter's writing said, "Well, we'll be going, Miss Rutledge. We'll see you later."

"Come back, children."

Easter watched them go, and Cloud could see the faint smile that lighted her face. "Good children," she said quietly.

"Nice to see you've found you some friends."

"Children are always the same—white children, Indian children . . ." He watched the sadness drift into her eyes again, and he knew she was remembering.

He pointed quickly to the slate. "Looks like you're doin' fine."

She looked at the letters she had made. "The Noconas have a picture writing, but it's not like this. Here you can write anything you want to say, any word." She looked away, to ward the children disappearing from sight. "It makes me feel foolish. I am so much older, yet they teach me."

Cloud smiled. Easter no longer had difficulty in talking. English had come back with use. Before long she would be reading and writing it.

"You're doin' fine," he said again. "Study with Hanna Lawton and pretty soon you'll be readin' and writin' a sight better than *I* can. I never had a chance for real schoolin' myself. Just had to pick it up the best way I could."

"I study and practice hard. It keeps my mind busy. I don't have so much time to think . . . about other things."

"But you *do* think about them."

The sadness lay dark in her face. Cloud knew it was never far beneath the surface. She said evenly, "I know it's useless, but there are things you can't forget. You even wake up, dreaming. . . ." She bit her lip. "Cloud, do you really think you'll find my family—my *white* family?"

Cloud nodded. "Maybe we will. The captain sent word down that way to see if there's still some Rutledges around."

"I hope there are. At first I didn't want to go. But now I want to see them. Maybe if I find a new home, new people, I can stop thinking so much. At least I can try, Cloud, I can try."

He saw then how much hope she was building up. She was grasping desperately for something to cling to.

"Do you think my people will be ashamed of me?" she asked worriedly.

"Ashamed? Why?"

Pensively she said, "I am a grown woman, but I don't know the things a white woman should know. I can't read, I can't write. I don't know much of the white man's God. Every day I make mistakes. All I know are the Indian ways. Maybe my family will be ashamed."

He reached out and took her hand. "Easter, don't you worry."

"Some people here have said I should be ashamed, living with the Indians when I am white, having an Indian husband. Do *you* feel that way, Cloud? Does that thought bother you?"

"Now, don't you fret yourself thataway," he said quickly. But his voice wasn't as firm as he wanted it to be. Truth was, it *did* bother him a little, even yet. He let go of her hand. "Easter, if they're your folks, they won't bother about what's past. They'll just take you and be glad you're back."

"I hope so," she said softly, "I hope so." She looked up at Cloud then, gratitude in her eyes. "You've been good to me, Cloud. I wish you could come here oftener."

"The captain keeps me awful busy."

"If he doesn't find any of my people, I won't have anyone, Cloud—no one but you and the Lawtons."

"You've got lots of friends here."

"It isn't the same as your own people." She looked down. "I hope they come soon. If they don't, I don't know how I can stand it."

"I been hopin' they wouldn't come *too* soon."

Her eyes narrowed. "Why not?"

"Because you'll be leavin' then, and I'll miss you."

She gave him a faint smile and touched his hand a moment. "I won't forget you, Cloud." She studied awhile, then asked unexpectedly, "If none of my people come, would *you* take me, Cloud?"

He stepped back, swallowing. "What?"

"I would have no husband, no people. A woman is not meant to be alone."

He stammered. "Look, Easter, among white folks . . ."

She nodded. "I know, they must have the papers and be married. It is like that among the Indians, except without the papers. But I would marry you. Would you marry me, Cloud?"

He swallowed again, and no words came. Hitting him that way all of a sudden . . . she hadn't learned the devious manner of the white woman yet. She still had the direct, devastating way of the Indian.

Looking down, she said, "Or maybe you wouldn't want to. Maybe you'd remember that before you there was an Indian husband."

Tightly he answered, "Easter, you're a good woman, a pretty woman. Any man'd be proud. The Indian husband hasn't got nothin' to do with it. It's just that I hadn't given no study to gettin' married, no study atall."

Yet even as he spoke, he knew he was half lying to her. He knew the thought of the Indian husband *might* stay with him. He knew this: that he wanted to reach out and pull her to him and kiss her. Yet he realized too that every time he touched her, he might remember there had been another man, a savage who had traded for her like he would swap for a brood mare.

He clenched his fist and wished to God he knew what to say.

As it was, he didn't get the chance to say anything. Captain Barcroft came striding down the creekbank toward him, his back straight, his dark eyes somber.

Cloud turned to meet him and stood half at attention. Half was about as far as he ever went. Figuring Barcroft was about to send him off on another long patrol, he asked wearily, "You lookin' for me, Captain?"

"Looking for both of you." The captain's eyes dwelt a moment on Easter Rutledge. Cloud saw no softness in them.

He hates that girl, he told himself.

Easter Rutledge stood up stiffly and faced the captain, her eyes turned suddenly hard.

And she doesn't like him any better, Cloud thought.

"What business do you have with me, Captain?" Easter asked, her voice crisp.

"I have some news for you, Miss Rutledge," the captain replied. "I've just gotten word that they've found a brother of yours down south. He'll be here in a few days."

Easter suddenly swayed. "A brother . . ." The words came in a whisper. She dropped her chin, and Cloud saw her lips go tight. She blinked, trying to stop a sudden rush of tears. Then she looked at the captain, her voice no longer steady.

"Only a brother? There are no others?"

The captain shook his head. "I couldn't say. The message spoke only of a brother."

Easter sat down limply in her chair. "My own people . . ." she said wonderingly. "My own people . . ."

Cloud took her hand and patted it gently. "That's sure fine news, Easter. I'm glad for you." But he knew he really wasn't. He felt something sinking inside him.

The captain turned his gaze to Cloud. "I'm afraid I have something for you too, Cloud. Miguel Soto has come in with a report of Indian signs—raiding party south of here. I'm preparing to take out the company."

Cloud nodded. "All right, sir. I'll be right with you."

The captain tipped his hat to the girl and said, "Good day," as if he had just casually met her strolling on the street. He turned on his heel and walked back up the creekbank.

Gripping Easter's hand, Cloud stood a moment looking down at this woman, wishing he knew something to say. But there weren't words for what he really felt.

"Easter," he spoke quietly, "I got to be goin'. But as to what you said to me a while ago—what you proposed—I felt honored that you asked me, sure enough I did. But I wouldn't go tellin' Mother Lawton about it, was I you. You see, white women sort of beat around the bush on things like that. They don't just come out plain that way. They get what they want from a man, but they make him think it was *his* idea. Mother Lawton might not understand."

Still dazed by the captain's news, Easter said, "I will remember. Be careful, Cloud."

"I will. And don't you go leavin' here till I get back."

He squeezed her hand, then turned away to follow the captain.

Eight

LANCING IN BELOW BRUSH HILL, THE INDIAN RAIDING party had struck out in an arc northeastward. Plenty of settlers in that direction, and plenty of horses. Good strategy for the Indians. Coming in from open country to the west, they could go out to the north without having to retrace their steps, without running head-on into aroused white pursuit.

The raid caught Barcroft's company short, many of his men out on scout and patrol duty. He sent quick word to those he could reach in short time. The others he would have to do without. To those who could get the message, he set a rendezvous point so the rest of the company would not have to wait in camp. Two hours after the alarm was raised, the company was riding out in a column of dry dust, spurs jingling, saddle guns jostling in leather scabbards. Silent men sat straight, shoulders squared, a battle-eagerness in their faces.

Out in the lead rode Cloud and Soto, the Mexican led by his unerring instinct even though they hadn't yet struck the trail. He knew which way it had headed—where they were most likely to cross it without riding unnecessary miles. He rode to it like a bee to the hive.

As the small company moved along, some of its men began catching up and falling in from other duty, adding strength. At the appointed rendezvous point, Barcroft called a short halt for rest. And while the men waited, others showed up as instructed.

Barcroft looked with Miguel and Cloud at the trail the Indians had left. "About fifteen of them, you think?"

"*Sí, mi capitán,*" said Miguel. Cloud nodded agreement.

The captain glanced back over his men and nodded in satisfaction. "Fair match, then, I'd say. Let's go."

The Indian tracks were several hours old, but the Rifles were pushing their horses as hard as they dared, yet saving strength for a long chase if it developed.

At length the company came upon a spot where the Indians had reined up and milled around as if in conference, then had scattered. Cloud raised his chin and sniffed. "Smoke, Captain, I do believe."

Barcroft took a long breath and replied, "You're right. Let's find it."

They rode out, and the smell grew stronger. Cloud glanced at Miguel, then swung his rifle around in front of him on the saddle, where he could get at it in a hurry. He could see the smoke now through a line of brush which clustered along a summer-dry watercourse. Breaking through the brush, he and Miguel saw the still-crackling ruins of a cabin, the roof tumbled in among the charred sidelogs. They reined up to give the scene a long look from some distance.

"Been a spell since they left, I reckon," Cloud commented in a moment. "We better look around; might still be somebody alive."

Even as he spoke, he saw a movement in the brush at the other side of the cabin. He gave the rifle a quick jerk, freeing its leather thong from the saddlehorn. Then he let the rifle ease down again.

"By Ned," he breathed. "A woman and kids."

From out of the brush came a woman and several children, a couple of them boys of ten to twelve. The woman carried a baby in one arm, a rifle in the other. One of the boys also held a rifle. The woman walked up to the two advance scouts as the rest of the company broke out of the timber behind them. She looked them over a moment before she spoke.

"Howdy. Be you fellers Rangers?"

Barcroft spoke, "We're the Mounted Rifles. It appears you've had some unwelcome company."

"Well," she replied slowly, "they wasn't invited."

"Anybody hurt?"

"No, sir, we taken to the brush in time. Husband, he was out cow-huntin', and he ain't got back yet. He's goin' to be some mad when he does git back. They got all the horses we had, 'cept the one he's on."

Barcroft said, "Do you have any neighbors you can go to?"

She nodded. "We got neighbors pretty close, only seven-eight miles. We'll go over there soon's my husband gits in." She frowned. "You don't reckon them *national assassinators*'ll be a-comin' back?"

That was a name some people on the frontier had given the Indians because of the federal reservation that had afforded some of the marauders sanctuary between raids.

Barcroft said, "I doubt they'll be back this way. They came in one direction, and I'd judge they'll go out another." He looked at her children, and Cloud could read the thought in the captain's troubled eyes. "Just the same, ma'am, I'd take care. It would be wise of you to move to a settlement and stay there."

She shook her head, much as Lige Moseley had done when the captain had made the same suggestion to him. "No, thank you, sir, we lived in one of them settlements once. There's things worse than Indians."

Barcroft shrugged. People like this, you couldn't scare off. "It's up to you. I wish we could stay and help, but we've got to keep moving."

"We'll make it all right."

"Maybe we'll recover your horses, ma'am. We'll try."

Moving out, they began to cross land that was vaguely familiar to Cloud. After a long time they broke out of the big thicket and came into sight of old Lige Moseley's double cabin. Cloud's heart quickened. The Indian trail led straight that way. They had hit Lige, too, sure as thunder.

The cabin was still standing, though Cloud hadn't seen any sign of life around it. He held up his hand to slow down the rest of the company until he had a chance to ride in and show himself.

"If that old fire-eater's still alive," he told Miguel Soto, "he's a crack shot. We don't want him makin' any mistakes."

Lige's dogs set up an awful racket as Cloud rode in alone. Lige Moseley stepped out from the corral, waving his left hand. His right hand was weighted down by a rifle big as a cannon. Cloud glanced over into the corral. Just as the last time, Moseley's horses were safe inside.

The settler's bearded face broke into a wide grin. "Well, you boys come too late. Excitement's done over."

Looking around, Cloud saw little sign of battle. These raiders evidently had been smarter than the last bunch.

They hadn't tried to go up against Moseley's solid walls. "Get you any Indians?"

Moseley shook his head. "Can't say as I did. But we didn't lose no horses, neither. Comanches has got to git up awful early in the mornin' to steal anything off of this outfit."

The rest of the company rode in after seeing it was all right. The captain, dusty now with whiskers beginning to darken his face, nodded at Moseley. Mrs. Moseley and the children filed out of the house to see the Mounted Rifles. The captain's gaze dwelt a long time on the children, especially on a little girl of three or so named Joanna.

Same age as his was, Cloud thought.

Barcroft said, "It appears you've been lucky again, Moseley."

"Ain't just luck, Captain," Moseley replied, patting his big rifle. "Keen eye down the barrel of one of these is better than luck. And keen eyes just naturally run in the Moseley family." He pointed his chin at his wife and at the boy Luke. "You-all care to stop and rest yourselves a mite?"

The captain shook his head. "Can't. The Indians lost a little time here, and they lost some at another place back down the way. If we *don't* lose any we'll be able to make some gain on them."

Moseley agreed with a nod of his head. "I'm a right fair shot, Captain. I'd be tickled to go along and he'p you, if you'd care to have me."

Barcroft shrugged. "Suit yourself. But what about your family?"

"Them Indians won't be back. Besides, Luke'll be here. He's as good a shot as I am."

While Lige saddled his horse, Samantha Moseley came farther out into the yard. She stood silently watching

Cloud, her eyes soft with a longing she probably could not even understand.

The dogs followed for a way as the company rode out. Cloud turned once in the saddle to see if they had dropped back. He saw Samantha still standing there, watching him.

Miguel Soto glanced at Cloud, his eyebrows raised. "Pretty girl, that one," he commented pointedly. "A most pretty girl."

The Indian trail was not hard to follow. Besides their own mounts, there were the several extra horses the Comanches had picked up. An hour or so from Moseley's, Cloud and Miguel, up front again, came across one of the Indian horses limping along painfully. Dirt was caked on its chest and along one side. It evidently had fallen and lamed itself, and its rider had transferred to one of the stolen horses.

"Still sweatin' a little," Cloud observed. "Them redskins ain't too awful far in front of us anymore."

Shortly afterward, he thought he heard the distant sound of gunfire, drifting in the north wind. He stepped out of the saddle and handed Miguel his reins. Then he walked out a little piece to listen, where squeak of saddle leather wouldn't bother him.

He listened a minute or two, turning his head first one way, then the other, his face drawn into a deep frown. "I'd of sworn I heard it," he said, shaking his head. He rode back to report it to the captain, then regained his lead with Miguel. "You ever hear anything, Miguel?" he asked.

The Mexican shook his head. "Maybeso you got better ears."

"Or a better imagination."

They were in and out of the brush for an hour before

they suddenly came in sight of a single wagon, sitting at the edge of a big post-oak motte. Part of its canvas cover had been burned away.

Cloud sucked in a short breath. "Caught 'em a mover. Bet they didn't leave much of him."

Then he saw movement at the wagon, and he got a glimpse of a man with a hat on, the quick flare of a skirt. "Looky there, Miguel. Them folks must of scrapped their way through it."

He spurred into an easy lope, Miguel close beside him. He reined up just short of the wagon and took a quick look. He saw one gray-bearded man and two women—one old like the man, one young. The man had his left arm wrapped in a white strip of cloth, evidently torn from a woman's underskirt. A blotch of red showed through it. The older of the women stood close, hand red with blood from the bandaging. The younger woman stood a little to one side, the clutch of fear still strong in her dust-smeared face.

Cloud dismounted, flipping his loop rein over his horse's head and keeping hold of it. "You folks must've put up a dandy fight to've run them off." He didn't say it, but he thought it would have taken a lot to have discouraged a bunch of bucks if they had seen the young woman. "You didn't lose anybody?"

The old man shook his head. "They got off with our team, but we got off with our lives."

Cloud glanced at a rifle leaned against the wagon wheel.

"That the only gun you got?" he asked incredulously. "Don't seem like one gun would've held them off long."

"We had a pistol too. Wife used the pistol."

Cloud glanced questioningly at Miguel. Three people with only two guns between them, and a prize like that young woman with her long brown hair. Didn't seem reasonable.

He looked at the household goods piled in the wagon and said, " 'Pears you folks was movin' someplace."

The old man nodded. "We was. But we can't git far now without horses."

The fear still lay live and fierce in the young woman's face. "Ma'am," Cloud said to her, "you don't need to be scared no more. They're gone, and I don't expect they'll be back."

She tried to speak, but the words stuck in her throat.

"My daughter-in-law, mister," the old man said quickly. "She got a bad scare. She'll be all right."

"Where's your son?" Cloud asked.

The old man hesitated, "Why, he's off in the army—the Confederate Army."

"And you was movin', just the three of you?"

"That's it, that's all there is to it." The old man was plenty nervous, and so was the old woman. Cloud thought that was natural, considering what they had just been through. And yet . . .

Then he saw the tracks, a set of boot tracks that didn't match the ones he saw around the old man's feet. And Cloud knew.

There was somebody else with this wagon!

Barcroft rode up with the rest of the company. As was his way, he wasted no time with foolish questions. "Nobody killed?"

The old man shook his head. "No, sir, no damage except a little scratch on my arm, and the fact that them red thieves run off with our horses."

Like Cloud, Barcroft found it hard to believe these three had stood off that raiding party alone. "How did you do it?"

The old woman spoke up for the first time. "We seen

them Indians comin' and knowed we couldn't outrun them. We got our wagon up here and piled off and took out into that brush yonder. They didn't try too hard to come in and git us. They just cut the team loose and left. They set the wagon afire, but we put the fire out before it did us much hurt."

The captain looked at the young woman, and he gently shook his head. Watching him, Cloud knew the captain was thinking the same thing the scout had.

The captain said, "How about showing us where you made your stand?"

The old man argued, "Now, soldier, there don't seem to be no reason for that. 'Pears to me like you fellers would be most interested in gittin' out after them Indians."

"I'd just like to see how you fought them off." Cloud could see suspicion in the captain's eyes.

Then Miguel bent over and examined the foot tracks. "*Capitán!*"

Catching Miguel's eye, Cloud quickly shook his head. But it was already too late. The captain said, "What is it, Miguel?"

Miguel glanced again at Cloud and shrugged. "It is nothing, *Capitán*. We forget it."

"You've found something," the captain pressed. "What is it?"

Hemmed up, Miguel showed Barcroft the tracks. The captain said grimly, "I knew something was wrong here. I just couldn't put my finger on it." He turned to the old man and pointed out into the brush. "Who's in there?"

Trembling, the old man said, "Nobody, sir, nobody. You're mistaken."

The captain declared, "There's no mistake. You're hiding someone. Who is it?" When he got no reply from the old man, he turned sharply to the young woman. "Your husband, perhaps? What is he, a deserter? A conscription dodger?''

Tears rolled down the young woman's cheeks, leaving trails in the dust that lay heavy on her face. ''Please,'' she begged, ''please.''

Barcroft turned to his men. ''Dismount and fan out. We'll push through that brush until we find him.''

Miguel eased up close to Cloud. Quietly he said, ''I'm sorry. I speak before I think.''

''Can't help it now.''

They moved out in a walk, a ragged line of men filtering through heavy brush. Cloud could hear the young woman sobbing behind them. She was following. He turned once and told her, ''Ma'am, you better go back.''

She kept coming, and he let her alone.

A jackrabbit jumped up and skittered away, and half the men in the group jerked their rifles up in sudden reflex before they realized what it was.

Then a man somewhere ahead of them shouted, ''Stay back, all of you! We've got rifles here!''

Cloud saw a movement. It wasn't one man; it was two!

''Stay back!'' the voice shouted again. There was a shot that clipped the leaves out of a post oak above Cloud's head. Then came the sound of a quick struggle and a second man saying sharply, ''Put the gun down. It's no use.''

Two men stood up in plain sight, their hands in the air. Cloud broke into a trot toward them. He was one of the first men to reach them. Behind him came the young woman, crying, ''Don't shoot them! Please don't shoot them!'' She dodged in front of Cloud and threw her arms about one of the men, sobbing. The man lowered his chin and pressed his cheek to her hair, his hand gently patting her back.

Barcroft moved up to them and said solemnly, "You're under arrest."

"What for?" one of the young men asked.

"Desertion, possibly, or flight to avoid conscription. Whichever it is, we'll find out."

The woman turned her face toward the captain. "What'll happen to them?"

Evenly the captain said, "They fired upon a Confederate company. I'd say they'll likely hang for that."

She cried out, "No!" and clung tightly to her husband.

The younger of the two men said, "I was the one fired the shot, not *him.* Besides, I didn't shoot at nobody. I just fired over your heads. Hoped I'd scare you off."

It was easy to tell that the two men were brothers, both in their twenties, both tall and strongly handsome with the broad shoulders of men who know well the ax and the plow.

"What happens to you will be up to a military court," Barcroft said.

Seward Prince growled, "Unionists, I'd bet, the both of them. Hangin'd be just about right, if you was to ask me."

Curtly Cloud said, "Nobody asked you."

The Rifles walked back out to the edge of the timber, with the two men in front of them and the young woman leaning tearfully against her husband. The old couple stood slumped helplessly, hopelessness in their tired, grieving faces. They sat down on their wagon tongue, and the old man pleaded:

"Captain, it weren't none of their fault. I was the one made them run. It's this damned war. It's not *our* war. We didn't ask for it, and we don't want no part of it. I got no slaves and don't want none. I say if these rich landowners and slave men want a war fought, let them fight it theirselves, and leave us poor folks alone!"

Cloud thought he could see sympathy in the captain's face, which surprised him a little. But he knew the captain was not one to be swayed from duty, even by sympathy. The captain asked, "Where were you going?"

"We was tryin' to git to Mexico."

"That's a long way."

The old man nodded. "It is that, but we had nothin' much else but time anyway. We wasn't goin' to hurt nobody. We was just tryin' to find us a neutral ground. Is that a sin, Captain?"

The captain slowly shook his head. "Too bad, old-timer. If your boys had stayed out in plain sight, we never would have thought much about it, might not even have asked any questions. But they hid, and that changed things. When they fired on us, that sealed the warrant. We'll have to take them with us."

The people were silent a moment. Then the old man asked, "And what about us? What're we goin' to do?"

The captain had no answer. Lige Moseley spoke up quietly: "I got a cabin south a-ways. Back-trail us, and you'll find it. If we don't git your horses back from the Indians, maybe I can swap you a couple. There's lots of things me and my family needs, and maybe you got some of it we can trade you out of."

While the two young men said their tearful good-byes to the family, the captain had a couple of packhorses stripped so the prisoners could ride them.

"You'll have to go bareback," he said to the pair, "but that's the best we can do. And we've got to take you with us because we can't spare anybody to stay back and guard you."

Lige Moseley frowned. "I'd guard them, Captain."

The captain smiled. "That's a kind offer, Moseley, but I don't know you that well. Being a friend of Cloud's, you might even share a little of his Unionist feeling, for all I know.'' Despite the smile, Cloud could tell the captain was dead serious. ''No offense, but I like to know my guards.''

Moseley turned his palms upward and shrugged.

They moved out again, quickly leaving behind them the wagon, the old man and the women. For as long as the raiders remained in sight, the trio watched motionless—three tragic statues standing in the grass.

The Indian signs were fresh now. Captain Barcroft signaled Cloud and Miguel to speed up. But darkness came, and the Indians had not been caught. Reluctantly, Barcroft called a night halt. The men ate supper and stretched out to rest. Barcroft had the prisoners' hands tied to the trunks of trees, and set a special guard to watch over them through the night.

Long before daylight, the men were up. As soon as they could see tracks, Cloud and Miguel were out a-horseback, far in the lead of the company.

Before long they came to the place where the Indians had camped. The ashes were still warm. Cloud nodded in satisfaction at Miguel, and the pair moved out. It wasn't hard now to keep the company at a strong pace. If anything, it was hard to hold them back.

Late in the morning Cloud and Miguel rode into sight of the Indians. They reined up quickly and gave the Indian sign to the company behind them. Barcroft spurred forward in a lope. He took a long look, then signaled the men to spread out and charge. The sound of pounding hoofs carried ahead to the Indians. Cloud could see the alarm rush through the bunch like the sudden sense of danger spreads through a herd of buffalo. The Indians pushed their horses into a hard run.

Way ahead of them lay a stretch of timber. The Indians made for it. Cloud spurred hard, the captain riding right along beside him. Glancing at Barcroft, Cloud could see the man's grim anticipation. Truly, here was a man who hated with all his soul, who took a fierce pleasure in seeing Indians die.

Realizing they could not make the timber, the Indians did a strange thing. They stopped and turned around, letting their stolen horses go. They formed a rough line and came running straight back toward the Rifles. Lances bristled. Cloud could see bows swung into readiness. He caught the glint of sunlight off a rifle barrel.

Most of the Texans drew their pistols, for this was going to be sudden and mean—and close up. With the pistol they would have six shots instead of the one they could get from a rifle.

One of the two prisoners pulled up beside the captain. "For God's sake, sir, give us a gun so we can defend ourselves."

Barcroft said something unintelligible, then there was no more time, for the Indians were upon them. The Indians fired first, arrows sailing ahead of them, flame blossoming from stolen guns. A Rifleman's horse went down, and Cloud heard a man shout in pain as an arrow plunked into a leg.

The Texans hauled up on the reins—most of them—and fired back with their pistols. A couple of Indian horses went down, and an Indian was chopped off of his mount as if he had run into the low limb of a tree. The rest of the Indian force passed by and went on beyond, carried by the momentum of the rush.

Suddenly, then, Cloud could see that the Rifle force had been scattered. The captain was far out to one side. The Indians wheeled their horses around and came back for another desperate try. An early shot from one of them brought the captain's horse down. Cloud saw the animal fall, saw the captain's gun sail out into the grass. The captain tried to slip out from under the animal, but he could not move. He was pinned.

Cloud yanked his horse around and spurred out toward the captain. But the oldest of the two prisoners was closer. He raced to the captain's side and stepped down from his horse, letting the mount run on without him. The prisoner grabbed up the captain's fallen gun and threw himself to his belly in the grass, beside Barcroft.

A handful of Indians, seeing the two men down, peeled off from the rest and swept down toward the pair. Cloud saw the prisoner grab the captain's rifle out of the saddle scabbard, even as he handed the captain the pistol. Leveling the rifle over the dead horse, the man took careful aim and fired just as the nearest Comanche drew a bow into line. The Indian rolled in the grass and went limp as an empty sack.

By the time Cloud got there and stepped off beside the captain, the Indians had hauled up. Cloud fired once, bringing down one of the horses. The Indian, left afoot, reached up for help and got it from one of his friends. He swung up behind another Indian and rode away.

It was a rout now, the remaining Indians abandoning the stolen horses and everything else in an effort to get to the timber.

Most of the Rifles followed after them awhile, managing to bring down one more. They stopped short of the timber, for that was likely to be like a beehive.

With his own horse and rope, Cloud managed to pull the captain's dead horse over and free Barcroft. The captain stood up shakily. The young prisoner loosened the cinch and got the captain's saddle loose.

That done, Cloud walked back to Barcroft and asked, "Everything all right, sir?"

Barcroft was rubbing his leg. "I guess. There doesn't seem to be anything broken." He glanced at the prisoner.

"I was in a bad spot for a minute," he said to the man. "If you hadn't come when you did, they'd have ridden over me, more than likely. And they wouldn't have left much."

The prisoner was trembling a little now, the nervous aftermath of the quick battle. He didn't say anything.

The captain observed, "It might have been better for you if you'd let them get me."

When the young man said nothing, Cloud put in, "Captain, it just goes to show you the kind of man he is. He couldn't let a thing like that happen to you, even if standin' back might've given him a chance to go free."

Barcroft said evenly, "Cloud, you should know better than try to change my mind."

"Wasn't tryin' to change nothin', Captain. I was only thinkin' maybe this might make you show some extra consideration."

"Damn it," Barcroft argued, "I'm a soldier. I can't allow personal feelings—personal gratitude—to stand in the way of my duty."

"Can't you, Captain? Ain't nobody knows about these boys but us. What other people don't know won't hurt them none."

The captain said sharply, "I already feel badly enough about this. Don't make it any worse for me." Turning away, he said to Miguel, "Take a few men and go bring that bunch of stolen horses up here. Some of us need remounts."

He walked on out across the grass, halting just once to look back.

Cloud said with satisfaction, "It's eatin' at him. That's a good sign."

The older prisoner said, "Truth of it is, Mister Cloud, I wasn't really thinkin' much about the captain when I done it. I could see that gun lyin' out there, and I didn't have one. I wanted that gun. I didn't care about the captain."

Cloud held down a grin. "For God's sake, don't you tell *him* that!"

Later that afternoon they came back by the abandoned wagon. Footprints showed the old man and the old woman had gone on to Moseley's, as suggested. The captain let the two brothers hook their recovered horses to the wagon and drive it. The company camped for the night at Moseley's place.

Several times Cloud saw the captain looking at the two brothers and their family. With Lige Moseley, he discussed the uncertainty he could see in the officer's face.

"Lige, I think he's about made up his mind. Only question is, how can he do it and get by with it. You got a couple of extra horses you'd be willin' to swap to that old man—a couple of *fast* horses?"

Lige Moseley pulled at his whiskers. "I don't want you gittin' the idea I go along with your Union leanin's, 'cause I don't. But I kind of took a likin' to them two boys." His white teeth showed in a smile. "I just *might* have a pair of horses, sure enough."

Presently the captain came over to Moseley. "Mister Moseley, yesterday you offered to guard our prisoners. I have a lot of tired men needing rest. Would you still consent to do it—to guard them tonight?" While Lige considered, the captain added pointedly, "Now, I wouldn't want you to go to sleep. Of course, you being a civilian, I couldn't do anything to you if you did. You *would* stay awake, wouldn't you?"

Lige grinned. "Sure, Captain. You can count on me to do what's right!"

Next morning Lige and Elkin walked up to the captain just at daylight and shook his shoulder. The captain turned over on his blanket and raised up on one elbow, blinking.

Lige said, "Captain, I'm afraid them two prisoners has gotten away!"

"Gotten away?" Barcroft asked with little show of surprise. "Now, I wonder how they did that?"

"Reckon I went to sleep, Captain, even after the promise I made you. Tireder than I really thought. Boys taken a couple of my horses and headed south. Must've gone sometime early in the night."

Elkin asked Barcroft, "Should we go after them?"

The captain shook his head, a shadow of a grin about him. "They have too much of a lead on us now. There'd be no use in it."

Elkin began to understand, humor playing in his eyes. "We *could* notify some of the companies to the south of us."

The captain looked at the smiling Cloud, then cut his gaze back to Elkin. "Yes, I guess we could. I'll write a letter to Austin—first time I think about it."

Nine

INDIAN RAIDS EXCEPTED, IT WAS ONE OF THE MOST exciting days Brush Hill had ever known. The word came in that Easter Rutledge's brother was due to arrive. Down at the Lawton house, Mother Lawton and Hanna and several other women bustled about in good-natured confusion, trying to get Easter prepared for the meeting. But if anything, they were just making her more and more flustered, more and more nervous.

Cloud went down to see what was happening and found Hanna working with Easter's hair while Mother Lawton sewed one of Hanna's dresses, taking it up to fit Easter. Other women were cooking up a feast—or such a feast as an isolated frontier community could ever have.

Looks like they're fixin' to feed fifty people, Cloud thought. *Ain't but one brother, is there?*

Without any patrol duty to perform, and somehow getting the feeling he was underfoot in all this feminine company, Cloud rode off down the south trail alone and took up a station in the shade of an oak. Loose-tying his horse, he sat on the ground. With one eye watching the trail, he idly sketched maps in the sand, then wiped them out and started over. This, to him, was a worthwhile pastime in that it helped firm in his mind the outline of the various parts of the country he had ridden in.

Tiring of his mapmaking, he finally settled down to watching the trail, looking for a sign of a rider. He asked himself a dozen times what kind of man Easter's brother would turn out to be. He asked himself if Easter would really be happy when she found her own family. Maybe she would. He had seen the glow in her eyes a while ago. She had been depending strongly upon this, for there was little else she *could* depend upon anymore. She had left so much behind her. . . .

Cloud almost wished they had never found her brother. Again and again her words came back to him: *Would you marry me, Cloud? Would you marry me?*

He clenched his fist. *Why didn't I tell her yes? Why couldn't I be man enough to forget about that Indian?*

Now, he knew, it was too late. This was a big country. Once she went south, chances were he would never see her again. He might not even be able to find her if he tried.

A man can be a fool sometimes. If he really loves a woman, he ought to be able to forget about everything else. Why couldn't I?

He saw the wagon a long time before it reached him, and somehow he knew this would be the man. Slowly he stood up and stretched himself, then stood stiffly and watched the wagon approach. As it neared, he stepped out away from the tree and toward the trail. He held up his hand.

The man hauled up on the lines and spoke to his team.

"Whoa, there, whoa-a-a." The dust from the wheels swirled up around him and then drifted out leisurely on the breeze from the north. The young man twisted his face at the taste of the dust, then turned toward Cloud and asked, "How much farther to Brush Hill?"

Cloud eyed him carefully, looking for some resemblance to Easter. "You're almost there." The man was perhaps a couple or three years older than Easter. He had the skin of a man used to staying indoors. Storekeeper, perhaps. But there was something about his eyes that showed he was related to Easter, no mistake about that. "Would you by any chance answer to the name of Rutledge?"

The young man nodded. "I would." He quietly looked Cloud over from head to foot. "And what might be your business with me?"

Cloud shrugged. "No business, I reckon. I just rode out to get the first look at you, and help you find your way in. Cloud's my name." He extended his hand. Rutledge hesitated, then took it.

"Kenneth Rutledge is mine. Ken, better known."

A vague reserve still held the man, as if he somehow distrusted Cloud. "Did they send you out to meet me?"

"Came on my own. I was the one found Easter . . . Miss Rutledge. Got kind of a special interest in her, I guess you'd say. Wanted to be sure her brother didn't have no trouble findin' where she's at."

Rutledge seemed to be looking a hole through Cloud. "You can stop worrying about her now, Mister . . . what was it . . . Cloud? She'll be my responsibility from now on."

Uncomfortable, Cloud stepped back. "Well, I expect you'll be wantin' to get on in to the settlement."

"It's been a long trip," Rutledge acknowledged. "But tell me, how does my sister look?"

Cloud blurted, "She looks mighty good to me." Then,

realizing how awkward that sounded, he corrected himself. "What I mean is, she's in good health. Folks here've taken fine care of her."

Kenneth Rutledge nodded. "That's nice of them," He looked ahead of him, up the trail. "Shall we go on?"

He doesn't think much of me, seems like, thought Cloud. "Sure," he said, "Why not?"

Rutledge started his team as Cloud walked back to his horse and swung into the saddle. Cloud spurred to catch up, then pulled his horse to an easy trot alongside the wagon.

"Kind of a surprise to you, I reckon," he spoke, "findin' out after all these years that she was still alive."

"A real shock. I'd given her up for dead—we all had—a long time ago. Ever since the word came, I've been wondering—worrying—how she was going to be."

"Well, you sure don't have to be a-worryin'. She's fine, and you can take my word for that."

Cloud felt Rutledge's eyes appraising him, and he got the notion Rutledge didn't accept his judgment as amounting to much.

I look a little like an Indian myself these days, he thought, seeking the reason. *All that ridin', all that sun . . .*

He pulled up at the Rifles' camp, and Kenneth Rutledge sawed on the reins, stopping his wagon. Looking at the man's dusty face, the dark shadow of whiskers, Cloud said, "I expect you'd like to clean up and maybe shave before you go on to see Easter."

Stepping down from the wagon, Rutledge said, "I'd appreciate it."

"I'll introduce you to Captain Barcroft. Then I'll ride on down and tell the folks you're here, so they can be ready."

Rutledge held back a moment. "Cloud, tell me one thing. Have the years in captivity done much to her? I mean, I've been wondering how she would fit in. We have a tight-knit little community back home now. Settled folks, churchgoing people. Good-hearted and all, but sort of set in their ways, you understand. Easter's going to be a real curiosity to them. They'll have their eyes on her." He frowned. "It wouldn't be her fault, of course, if she made a few mistakes right at first. After all those years among the savages . . . you couldn't expect perfection."

An oddly cold feeling touched Cloud's stomach. "Don't you worry none about Easter. She'll do fine."

The women could tell by the look on Cloud's face as he walked up to the Lawtons' door.

"He's here?" Mrs. Lawton asked, her hands clasped tightly against her bosom.

Cloud nodded. "Yes'm, he's here."

Other women began to talk all at the same time and ask so many questions he couldn't keep up with them. Cloud looked about for Easter and found her standing toward the back of the room, face pale from excitement. Her lips were drawn tightly against her teeth, and she was making a strong effort not to cry. She smiled a weak smile at Cloud, but she could not hold it long.

Cloud walked to her. He wanted to take her hands in his, but not in front of all this company. Besides, what good would it do now? She would be going soon. "Easter," he said, "he'll be along directly. He stopped off at the camp to clean up a little."

It was a painful effort for her to speak. "Cloud, what is he like?"

Cloud shrugged. "He's your brother. He looks a little like you."

"Is he nice?"

Cloud hesitated. "Why . . . he'd have to be, bein' your brother."

Easter looked around for a chair and sank into it. Cloud

could see she was trembling. She said, "Stay here, will you, Cloud?"

"Sure, I will, Easter. Just as long as you want me."

Mother Lawton came over, trembling as badly as Easter. "Now, child, don't you be nervous." The absurdity of her own words struck her funny, and she began to laugh. Easter laughed too, and some of the tension was gone. Mother Lawton took Easter's hand and patted it fondly. "Everything's going to be all right, you watch."

Easter said weakly, "I know. I won't be nervous."

The old woman kept patting Easter's hand. Cloud watched her and thought, *Thank God for a woman like Mother Lawton. It would be a poorer country without her.*

Hanna Lawton stayed close to the front door, watching. It seemed like hours before she turned and said tensely, "They're coming. Aaron's bringing him."

Cloud saw Easter stiffen. Quietly he spoke to her. "Easy now, girl." Mother Lawton stood up and took Easter's hands, gently pulling the girl to her feet. The old woman tried hard to smile and reassure Easter, but she had begun trembling again herself.

Aaron Barcroft stepped through the door, glanced quickly around, then made a sweeping motion with his hand, bidding Kenneth Rutledge to enter. Hat in hand, Rutledge walked in. His blue eyes made a rapid search around the hushed room, then fell upon Easter. His tongue came to his lips, and his chin quivered. He said almost in a whisper, "Easter?"

The girl tried to answer, but no sound came. She lifted her slender hand to her throat, then nodded. The hand shook. Her head went back a little, and the tears broke.

Kenneth Rutledge strode slowly across the room toward her. At arm's length he stopped a moment, looking down at the girl. Then he put his arms around her and pulled her against him, dropping his hat to the rough wooden floor.

Cloud turned and stared out the open window, his throat drawn into a knot. He heard Mother Lawton move slowly to the wall beside him. She was looking up at a framed picture of Jesus.

"Thank the Good Lord," he heard her breathe. "Thank the Good Lord!"

Most of the crowd had gone. Darkness had come, and the Lawtons and their company sat in the front yard, enjoying the coolness of the night. Henry Lawton and Mother Lawton sat in the chairs on the porch. Easter and her brother had pulled chairs out into the yard. Captain Barcroft stood to one side, Hanna Lawton near him, stealing glances at him.

Cloud sat on the ground, a stick in his hand, idly scratching marks that he couldn't even see. He was unusually edgy, knowing Rutledge was about to take Easter away. He watched the captain and Hanna.

If the captain had any imagination atall, he'd take Hanna for a walk, he thought. *That's what she wants. What does it take to make him see?*

Kenneth Rutledge was talking quietly. "There aren't but two of us left now, just my sister Flora and me. And Easter here makes three, of course. Mother died several years ago. Can you remember Mother, Easter?"

"A little. Just a little."

"She never was quite the same after the Indian raid. The rest of us gave Easter up for dead a long time ago, but not Mother. To the last day she lived, she said Easter was still alive. Got tired of listening to her sometimes. I guess a parent never can really give up."

Cloud glanced quickly at Aaron Barcroft and saw him draw up a little. Hanna touched the captain's arm.

Kenneth Rutledge said, "I was about nine or ten when it happened. You were about six, weren't you, Easter?" When Easter appeared confused, he said, "Of course you wouldn't know anymore. I don't suppose time means much in an Indian camp."

Irritably Cloud thought, *It'd mean a lot if you was a captive!*

"Yes," Rutledge went on, "I was about nine or ten. I stayed home that day to chop wood. Dad and our older brother went out afoot to work on a rock fence they were building. Easter wasn't supposed to follow after them, but she did. First we knew of the Indians was when we heard shots. Mother hustled Flora and me into the house and barred the door. I guess she knew, even then, that the others weren't coming back. She got down the old rifle, and she took up a stand by the window.

"After a little while the Indians came to the house a-horseback. They wanted in, but they could see Mother there with the rifle. They shouted threats at her, but she poked that gun out, and they knew she meant business. Then—I'll never forget it—they brought up Easter. One of them had her in front of him on a horse. And they had two fresh scalps. They waved them around and made signs like they were going to take Easter's scalp, too.

"It broke Mother's heart, but she couldn't help Easter, and she couldn't let them in. They'd have murdered us all if she had. None of those Comanches wanted to be the one she killed with that rifle. So finally they left, and took Easter with them. Neighbors followed their trail later, expecting to find Easter's body somewhere along the way. They never did, but everybody told Mother she was bound to be dead."

He turned to his sister. "I'm glad they were wrong."

Mother Lawton spoke from the porch. "So are all of

us. You've got a wonderful sister there, Mister Rutledge. You'll be proud of her."

Cloud asked something that had been bothering him all day. "What kind of plans you got for her, Mister Rutledge?"

"No real plans, Cloud." No *Mister* there. "I'll just carry her home and more or less let nature take its course. I'm sure there are lots of things she'll have to learn after spending all those years among the savages. Between Flora and my wife and I, I'm sure we can teach her. And, after a proper time, we'll begin introducing her around. That country is settled up, and there are lots of eligible men down there now. Who knows?"

Cloud clenched his fist. "You say *after a proper time*. You mean you're aimin' to keep her hidden till you're sure she's civilized enough to meet folks?"

Cloud's impatient tone drew a spark from Rutledge. "I didn't say that. What I said was . . . well, we want to be sure that she's ready before we take her out into public too much and risk embarrassing her. It's for her own good. Later on, then, she'll have nothing to look back to in shame."

Fist still clenched, Cloud wished he had voice for some of the angry thoughts that raced through his mind.

Not hard to tell he wouldn't like her associating with the likes of me.

Captain Barcroft had said little this evening. Much of the time he had spent just looking at Kenneth Rutledge, as if trying to gauge the man. At length he cleared his throat and spoke:

"There's one thing about your sister that I doubt anyone has told you yet, and I think you should know it."

Cloud felt it coming, and he steeled himself. *Why doesn't he keep quiet? Rutledge will find out soon enough anyway.*

Rutledge sat up straight, glancing sideways at Easter.

He saw Hanna turn away from the captain, and he was instantly suspicious. "What is it, Captain?"

Barcroft frowned at Hanna and hesitated a moment, evidently wondering how best to say it. "It's a thing you've probably considered already but haven't wanted to ask about. Your sister is a grown woman, an attractive woman, and she's long past marriage age from an Indian viewpoint."

The captain paused again, and Rutledge cast another wide-eyed glance at the silent Easter. "Captain, are you trying to tell me . . ."

Barcroft nodded. "She had an Indian husband!"

Cloud pushed himself to a stand. He put in angrily: "It wasn't none of her fault, Rutledge. Woman don't have nothin' to say about it. He bought her like you'd buy a heifer. He swapped a string of horses for her. She couldn't help it!"

Rutledge sank back in his chair, face twisted. He didn't say anything for a while. Then: "I guess I realized somehow that it had probably happened, but I didn't let myself think about it." He looked at Easter a long moment. "Easter, you *couldn't* help it, could you?"

Easter had her hands clasped tightly, and she was looking straight ahead, into the darkness, frozen motionless. "It was the Indian way."

Rutledge rubbed his forehead, trying to puzzle his way through. "I don't suppose we have to tell anybody. What they don't know . . ."

Barcroft said, "There's one more thing. The word will get out sooner or later, so it's best to start with the whole truth. She bore a baby by that husband."

Rutledge seemed to wilt. "A baby?" He shook his head, trying to reject the thought. "An *Indian* baby?"

The captain said, "That's right."

Rutledge didn't look at anyone for a while. He just sat

there as if he had been struck by the flat side of an ax. Finally he asked weakly, "Where is it?"

For a moment Cloud feared Easter would break down and cry. But she didn't. She sat stiff and silent, unblinking.

The captain said, "We left it behind."

Rutledge had his eyes closed. A long breath escaped him, and he said, "Thank God for that!" His hands trembled a little as he swayed forward in the chair. "But people will find out anyway. They always do about something like that. What're we going to tell them? How can we ever explain?"

Cloud moved forward stiffly, stopping beside Easter. "They're frontier folks, ain't they? They'll understand."

Rutledge shook his head. "The frontier passed us by a long time ago. We live in a settled community. We have churches now, and church people. They live by the Book."

Cloud gritted, "And don't that Book tell about Christian charity? The Lawtons here, they're Bible-readin' folks, and they understood. They never held nothin' against Easter, not for a single minute."

Rutledge didn't even seem to hear him. "How will I ever explain this?" he said, almost pleading. "What can I ever tell them? The name of Rutledge means something there. We've *made* it mean something. But what will it mean after this?"

Fists tight, Cloud stepped in front of Rutledge. "What kind of a man are you?" he demanded. "Here you've got a sister who's been through hell, and you're not even thinkin' of *her*—you're only thinkin' about yourself!"

Rutledge sat back in his chair, drawn up within himself, something akin to panic holding him in a tight grip. Finally he said, "You can't blame me. If I'd only known, if I'd even thought . . . You have to admit, it's an awful shock to spring on a man all of a sudden, an awful shock.''

I got a worse one I'd like to spring on you! thought Cloud. *But it'd hurt her as much as it would you. . . .*

Rutledge stood up shakily and got a grip on himself. Without a glance at Easter, he said to the others, ''I'm going back to the camp. I'm tired, and I have a lot to think about.''

Mother Lawton asked anxiously, ''We'll see you tomorrow?'' Rutledge only nodded without looking back as he walked out the gate.

Mother Lawton quietly arose from her chair on the porch. She walked out and stood by Easter, her hand on the girl's shoulder. ''It's all right, Easter,'' she said quietly, ''it's all right.''

Hanna Lawton leaned against the cabin wall, face buried in her arms. She turned to Barcroft and demanded tearfully, ''Aaron, how could you do it?''

The captain replied, ''It wasn't easy, but it had to be done.''

Hanna cried ''It didn't! It didn't!'' She whirled away from him and ran into the cabin. Barcroft took a step after her, his face unreadable in the darkness. Cloud heard him call, ''Hanna!'' Then he turned around without speaking to anyone else. He walked out the gate, following Kenneth Rutledge.

Next morning, while Cloud sat cross-legged on the ground cleaning his rifle, the captain walked up to him. Cloud gave the captain a quick glance but no greeting. He kept working with the rifle.

''Cloud,'' said Barcroft, ''I'm afraid I have to give you an unpleasant duty this morning.''

Ain't the first one, Cloud thought darkly, still angry about last night.

"Go down to the Lawtons' house and tell Easter Rutledge that her brother has gone!"

Cloud almost dropped the rifle. He set it down on a blanket he had spread out before him. He stood up stiffly and said, "Gone?"

"Got up before daylight, caught his team and left."

Cloud's lips were suddenly dry. "You sure he didn't take Easter?"

"Guard watched him leave. He didn't stop anywhere. He headed straight south."

"That dirty . . ." Cloud bit his lip and looked off toward the Lawton house, which was well out of sight. "And what about Easter? What happens to her now?"

The captain had no answer.

Cloud turned on him angrily. "It was your fault! You didn't have to tell him!"

Barcroft shook his head. "I had to tell him. Before I had talked with him twenty minutes, I knew what kind of man he was—a narrow-minded, egotistical fool."

Cloud thought, *Now look who's callin' somebody narrow-minded!*

Barcroft said, "I knew right then what he was likely to do when he found out. Better to have it happen here than on down the road somewhere, or back in her own town. At least here she has some friends."

Angrily Cloud charged, "You did it to spite her! You're as bad as Rutledge. You've had a contempt for her right from the first! You've hated her all along!"

"*Hated* her?" The captain seemed surprised at the thought. "Cloud, I never hated that girl. What gave you the idea I did?"

"The way you've treated her, the way you've avoided her. The times you've been over to the Lawton house, you haven't even looked at her. You've turned your head away. From the day we found her, you've wanted to be rid of her. If that's not hatred—if that's not contempt—I'd like to know what is!''

Barcroft sank to his heels and looked off into the distance. ''It wasn't hatred, Cloud, or contempt. I've felt nothing but pity for her.''

''Then why have you made it such a point to avoid her?''

Pain came into the captain's face. ''Because of the things I saw in her every time I looked at her, Cloud. Things I wanted to put out of my mind but couldn't when she was around. I looked at her and I saw my own daughter. I thought to myself, my daughter—if she's still alive—will live the same life this girl has lived. She'll grow up a savage, as much a Comanche as if she had been born one, and she'll know no better, just as this girl knew no better. When her time comes, she'll take a Comanche husband, just as this girl did. And she'll bear his children, Cloud—my own daughter—bearing his children just like any red-skinned squaw!''

Cloud saw the bleakness of prairie winter in the captain's dark eyes. After a long while he spoke. ''Captain, I'm sorry for anything I said to you.''

The captain said, ''You'd better go tell Easter.''

Ten

EASTER SAT IN HER ROCKING CHAIR, DRY-EYED BUT stunned as Cloud told her. Cloud shifted restlessly from one foot to the other, knowing her torment, knowing how she struggled to beat back the tears. He wanted to touch her, wanted to reach out and take her in his arms and shield her from hurt. But he couldn't shield her from this. He couldn't even help.

"Easter," he said quietly, "I know you've come to depend on findin' your family, to make up for what you'd already lost. But it don't mean the world's come to an end."

Face stricken, Hanna Lawton had walked out of the room when Cloud started to tell Easter what had happened. Mother Lawton stayed. Now she moved to Easter's side and spoke gently, "The young man's right, Easter. You've got friends here, and a home just as long as you want it."

Easter gave no response. Cloud put his hand over hers and said, "Easter, remember what we were talkin' about the other day? *I'll* give you a home, and I'll give you a family too. I want you to marry me, Easter!"

Cloud sensed Mother Lawton's approval, but he didn't glance at the woman. He looked down tensely at Easter, wondering if she had even understood. "Easter," he said again, "I want to marry you."

Presently Easter said in a hollow voice, "Because you feel sorry for me?" She shook her head. "I don't want it to be that way."

"It's *not* that way. I *want* to marry you. I love you, Easter!"

"A few days ago I asked *you,* and you said no. Nothing's changed since then, except that now you feel sorry for me." Again she shook her head. "Thanks, Cloud, for asking. But now *I'll* say no."

"Easter . . ." He realized then that it wouldn't help to argue with her now. Maybe later, when time had eased the hurt.

Easter said, "Cloud, would you please leave me alone now? I have a lot of thinking to do."

He squeezed her hand. "Sure, I understand. I'll come back tonight. Maybe by then you'll see your way through. And Easter"—he lifted her chin and looked into her desolate eyes—"Easter, please think about what I said. I *do* love you."

Outside, Hanna Lawton stood on the porch, a handkerchief gripped in her hand. Tightly she asked, "What now, Cloud? What now?"

He shoved his hands deep into his pockets and stood with his bleak gaze to the ground. "I don't know, Miss Hanna, I swear I don't."

"Aaron caused this," she spoke bitterly. "He's caused all her misery. Why couldn't he just have left her where he found her? She'd have been better off!"

"The captain never has done anything he didn't believe was right."

Odd, he thought, that he should ever find himself having to defend the captain to Hanna Lawton.

She demanded, "What ever gave him the idea he had the right to decide for others, a man who hasn't even been able to find his *own* way?" She choked and brought the handkerchief to her face again. "I wish I'd never seen him!"

Cloud said, "No you don't, not really. Maybe one day he'll see *you!*"

She looked up quickly, but Cloud walked away.

He went back that night. Hanna Lawton met him at the door, her face grave. He found all the Lawtons strangely quiet. "What's the matter?" he asked, alarm rising in him. "Where's Easter?"

"She's down by the creek," Hanna Lawton spoke, almost in a whisper. "She wants you to go down there."

Henry Lawton arose from his chair and drew on his pipe, his brow furrowed with worry. "Cloud, we've had a long talk with her. We don't like what she wants to do, but we can't talk her out of it. Maybe you can." He took the pipe out of his mouth and stared at it. "But if you can't, then for God's sake help her. She can't do it alone."

"Do what?" Cloud felt the blood draining from his face.

"Just go talk with her, Cloud."

He hurried down the creekbank, running into a cottonwood limb and knocking his hat off. He went down on one knee, then pushed to his feet again. "Easter," he called. "Easter, where are you?"

He heard her voice to his right, a calm voice. "I'm over here."

He found her sitting in the willow chair, staring out across the creek. "Easter," he said, the excitement riding high in him, "what're they tryin' to tell me? What is it you want to do?"

She turned to him, and he saw that her face was calm, the calmest it had been in a long time. "I've done a lot of thinking today. I've made up my mind. Cloud, I'm going home!"

"Home?" He sucked in a short breath, and he knew what the Lawtons had been trying to say.

"I've been trying to fool myself. I've thought if I could find myself a family, I could forget all I left behind. I found that family, and it wouldn't have me. It *wasn't* my family, I can see that now. They weren't really my people, not anymore. My real family is that baby, Cloud, and it's far up on the plains somewhere. My people are there, too, the only real people I have. So I'm going back to them. I'm going home."

He took her hands and held them tightly. "You're tired, Easter, and you're all upset. You're not thinkin' straight."

"I'm thinking straighter than I have in a long time. It's the only answer, Cloud, the only way."

"Easter, listen to me—"

"I *have* listened, and I've thought over all you said. But now I'm listening to my heart. And it says, go find that baby."

She leaned toward him. "I think I love you, Cloud. If things were different, maybe . . ." She shook her head. "But they're not, and there's no use talking about it now. I'm going home."

He lowered his chin. "Easter, have you thought what a terrible long way it is?"

"I have. It won't be easy."

"Alone out there, a woman, in that big country? You'd never find your way."

"Once I get onto the plains, I think I know the watering places. I've traveled with the tribe. I'll find them."

"Some stray Indian see you, he'll shoot you for a white woman without ever knowin' the difference."

"No," said Easter, "up there I won't be a white woman. I'll be Comanche. I didn't throw my Indian clothes away."

"You've lived long enough here to get to feeling the white man's way. Do you think you can live again like an Indian?"

"To find my baby, I'll live any way I have to."

"Would you take another Indian husband?"

"Not by choice."

"What if you had no choice?"

She shook her head in determination. "I want my baby."

"I won't let you do it, Easter!"

"How will you stop me? Chain me to a post? You may stop me once; you might stop me twice. But sooner or later I'll find a horse, and I'll get away. Don't try to stop me, Cloud. One way or another, I'll go!"

Defeat lay heavy in Cloud. "If I can't stop you, I guess I won't try. And talkin' won't do any good either, will it?"

"No."

"Then I'll go with you!"

She stiffened. "Cloud—"

"No, don't try to talk me out of it. If you're goin', I'll go with you as far as I can."

Fear colored her voice. "The Indians will kill you!"

"I won't go all the way. But I'll stay with you till I know you can make it in alone."

"Cloud, please—"

"Hush, Easter. If you go, then I go too."

Resigned, she asked, "When?"

"Tonight, if you're ready. If we wait, the captain may send me out on a patrol." He knew that in such an event Easter would try to ride off and leave him.

"What about the captain? What'll he do when he finds you gone?"

Probably order me shot on sight, he thought. But he said, "I don't know. I guess I'll find out. Now you go get ready, throw together the things you need. I'll be back directly with a couple of horses."

As he started to turn away, she rose from the chair and caught his hand. "Cloud." He stopped and faced her. She said, "You're a foolish man." She turned her face up, stepped to him and kissed him. "But I *do* love you."

After Cloud came with the horses, Henry Lawton regretfully helped him put together a sackful of supplies from the store. Tying a string around the top of the sack, he stared gravely at it and said, "Too bad we got no dried beef to let you take. You're goin' to need it."

Cloud said, "There'll be game enough, I reckon. We won't be hungry."

Lawton drew on his pipe and cast a worried glance at Easter. Dressed in her buckskin clothes, her brown hair in braids again, she stood silently by the closed door, barely touched by the weak glow of the lamp. "You couldn't talk her out of it?" he asked.

Cloud shook his head. "Tried."

"How'd you get the horses?"

"Told the guard the captain had given me orders to go out on scout. No trouble there."

"Be trouble when you get back. Aaron'll want your hide."

Cloud reached for the sack, gripping it so tightly that the cords stood out on the back of his hand. "I know, but

I'll just have to face that storm when I get to it. I got another worry right now.''

''I'll tell Aaron I advised you to take her back. Maybe that'll help some.''

Cloud shook his head. ''Not likely. The captain's got a strong mind. Whatever he sets it to, that's the way things've got to be.''

Henry Lawton bit down hard on the stem of the pipe and leveled his gaze at Cloud. ''There's one way out, Cloud. You don't have to come back.''

Cloud straightened. ''You mean run?''

Lawton turned up his hands. ''Not run, exactly, just not come back. Head west to New Mexico or Arizona—even California. This war keeps on, it's goin' to be more and more unhealthy for a man with Union sympathies anyhow. You watch, before this thing's over there'll be burnin' and lynchin' and the like. The smart man would git!''

Cloud swung the sack over his shoulder. ''Texas is my home.''

''Just advice, Cloud. It don't cost you nothin', and you don't have to take it.''

Easter said a tearful good-bye to Mother Lawton and Hanna while Cloud put her Comanche saddle on her horse. Then she and Cloud rode out across the creek and headed northwestward.

They rode steadily through the night and all the next day, slowing down only occasionally to let the horses rest. Cloud turned periodically in the saddle to look over the back trail.

''You never know about the captain,'' he told Easter. ''We got to keep ridin' and put a lot of miles behind us. If he decided to come after us, he'd let Miguel do the trackin'. That Mexican could trail the shadow of an eagle clear across a mountain.''

Before them stretched the great brown vista of the

lower plains, swelling and falling gently beneath the late-summer sun, a dry land begging for rain, the smell of fire clinging to the scorched carpet of brittle grass. In vain they searched for a waterhole that hadn't long since dried up in the summer drought. The horses had slowed. Cloud's mouth was so dry that his lips were cracking. But he was saving the short canteen of water he had, saving it for Easter.

"Somewhere way up yonder," said Easter, "is a spring that flows all the time; good, clear water. If we could find it, I'd have no trouble getting home. I've been there several times, and I know the trail. But down here, this land all looks the same to me."

"To me, too," Cloud admitted glumly. Here he had only his frontiersman's instinct to depend on, and he hated to trust it with his life. True, it hadn't often been wrong. But it only took once. . . .

So weary they could hardly climb down from their saddles, they stopped to make camp a while before dark. Cloud found a spot where a buffalo bull had pawed out a hole, and he built a small fire there so it would not spread out into the dry grass. He had picked up dead limbs of a mesquite at a dried-out natural lake a couple of hours earlier and had tied them behind the saddle. Firewood was scarce in this country.

At a prairie-dog town he had managed to bring down one animal and recover it. Actually, he had shot a couple more, but they had rolled back down their holes so he couldn't get their bodies.

He had gutted the animal at the time. Now he finished skinning it and spitted the tiny carcass on a stick, holding it out over the fire.

"Hungry?" he asked the girl. She sat on the ground, legs gathered up, head against her knees. She nodded. "A little. Mostly I'm tired."

By the time the prairie dog was done, Cloud saw that Easter was dozing. Gently he shook her shoulder. She looked up, startled. Then she eased again and smiled at him.

"Supper's ready," he said. "It's not much, but it beats grass."

The animal wasn't large enough to satisfy the hunger of either one, much less both of them. There were some dried biscuits in the sack, and Cloud handed a couple of these to Easter. He started to take one for himself, then changed his mind and dropped it back into the sack.

Things might get worse instead of better, he thought. He'd keep these for Easter. Instead of the biscuits he munched on a few dry mesquite beans he had picked up earlier. He hated the taste of them. Far as he was concerned, they were meant for horses, not for men. But they could keep a man from starving to death.

Finishing the meager supper, Easter took a small drink of water from her canteen while Cloud pushed dirt over the fire to put it out. He didn't want to risk its being seen in the darkness. But if anyone had followed after them, he'd be having the same kind of trouble. That, at least, evened things up.

By the time Cloud got through, he saw that Easter had stretched out in the grass, her blanket beneath her and her head on the saddle. He picked up his own saddle and blanket, and he was conscious of the girl watching him, wondering where he was going to put them. He walked out away from her a few feet and spread the blanket, then put the saddle down and eased his long frame wearily to the ground.

"Good night, Easter," he said.

In the gathering darkness he thought he could see her smile as she answered, "Good night."

With dawn they were up and riding again. For breakfast

they had eaten a little cold bread and had broiled bacon on a stick. Cloud had used enough of the remaining water to boil each of them a little coffee.

Into the hot day they rode, the sun climbing on their right, burning ever more relentlessly as the day wore on. Still no water. The horses were suffering now. Cloud picked up his canteen and shook it. He heard the slosh of the meager supply of water. "How much left in yours, Easter?"

"About the same," she said.

"We're goin' to have to let the horses have some of it, or we're liable to find ourselves afoot."

Dismounting, he took off his hat. He pushed the crown down and poured water into it. He held it up to his horse's nose. The horse quickly drank. Cloud repeated for Easter's horse. He could tell the horses wanted more, much more.

"Sorry, boys," he spoke, "that's all we got for you."

He shook his canteen again. Hardly any left. Easter was staring at the canteen, her lips tight. Cloud handed it to her. "You just as well finish it," he told her. "It'll evaporate anyway." It really wouldn't, in that tight canteen. But he could tell she badly needed a drink.

"What about you?" she asked.

"I'm used to it, goin' on these long scouts. And you've lived a white woman's life long enough to get spoiled." He smiled thinly and looked northwestward. "Somewhere yonder there's got to be water. We'll never find it standin' here."

He swung back into the saddle, lips burning and his body aching for the drink he hadn't let himself have. He touched heels to his horse, and the animal grudgingly started walking.

Late in the day he came upon the first sign: a pair of mesquite trees alone out here in these open plains. It wouldn't be too far to a waterhole, he figured. Where there were mesquites, water could usually be found someplace. Reason was that mesquites were most commonly spread by the wild mustangs which roamed these plains. Left alone, the horses never strayed too many miles from water. They ate mesquite beans from trees around the watering places. These beans later were spread out on the prairie, to sprout and grow more trees.

Presently Cloud came across a thin, almost invisible old buffalo trail, nearly grassed over. His heart gave a glad leap. He pointed it out to Easter and said, "The only question is, do we go up the trail or down it?"

Easter frowned. "There's another question, too."

"What's that?"

"Is there still water in the hole, or has it dried up like the others?"

He took a chance and decided to go up the trail. It angled westward, not far off their regular course. It was a very old trail, not used in a long time. But even when it was hard to spot beneath his horse's feet, he could see it meandering along ahead of him, a tiny thread of shadow in the dry grass.

At last he saw the cluster of mesquites far ahead of him. He grinned, though it hurt his parched lips. "Yonder it is," he pointed. "Just you hold on a while longer."

The horses plodded along in a walk, and it took them a long time to reach the place. Ahead, Cloud could see the small natural basin that caught the runoff from the rains, the runoff that would seep clear and clean from this heavy mat of protective grass.

He reined up on the rim of the basin and felt his heart plunge.

Dry!

He looked back at Easter, who had fallen behind. He felt a wave of pity come over him. How many times, traveling with the nomadic Comanches, had she come up thirsty to a waterhole like this and found the sun had drained it dry? Many times, no doubt. Yet each time it made a person die a little inside. It was something you never got used to. Thirst was worse than hunger. You could hitch up your belt a little and think of something else. When you were thirsty, your mind dwelt always on water.

He saw the bitter disappointment shadow her face.

Then he looked out across the dry lake and got an idea. "There's still a little green out in the middle of it, Easter. Maybe there's water there yet, under all that dried mud."

"It'll be bad water," she said.

"But it'll be wet."

He wished for a shovel, but that was one thing he hadn't thought to bring. Digging into his pack, he found a tin cup. This in hand, he walked out into the dry lake. In the center, where the grass and weed growth still showed some green, he dropped to his knees and began to dig.

It was slow, but after a while he found mud. Digging farther, he found water seeping into the hole as he took the mud out. He kept digging until he had made a hole about as deep as he could reach with his arm.

He raised up then, breathing hard from his exertion in the hot sun. The dank odor of the mud upset his stomach a little. Easter sat in the lacy shade of one of the mesquites watching him. He walked to her and flopped down on the ground.

"Got a slow seep workin'," he said. "We'll have to boil it before we can drink it, and even then we'll have to hold our noses. But it's water, and maybe it'll do till we can find somethin' better."

He boiled the water in a small bucket he had brought, then took the first swallow to be sure it wasn't poison. It wasn't, but it couldn't have tasted much worse if it had been. Involuntarily he spat out the first mouthful and exclaimed, "Damn!" He wiped his mouth on his sleeve.

Then he handed the cup to Easter. It was gyppy water which would leave them feeling almost as thirsty as before. But it was wet, and it would take care of the body's needs. After they had drunk all they could stand of it, he boiled enough to fill the canteens. The horses didn't like the water, either, but they drank it as Cloud poured it into his hat.

They rode on awhile. That night they made another dry camp. They did better for supper, because Cloud had shot a couple of rabbits near the lake. With darkness, they lay down again on the grass, their blankets apart. Cloud felt thirst working at him again, but he didn't want to open the canteens. They might need them far worse tomorrow.

He said, "The hell of it is that in this country we could pass by only a mile or two from water and never know it. Never been people up in this country much."

"There've been Indians here," she corrected him.

"I wasn't countin' them."

With a little of accusation in her voice, she said, "The white man *never* counts the Indian. Never thinks of him as human."

"Does the Indian think of the white man as human?" Cloud asked. "He couldn't, or he wouldn't kill and butcher the way he does."

Sadly Easter replied, "That's the whole trouble, I guess. I can see it now, because I've been on both sides. The Indian doesn't know anything about the white man's way and doesn't care to learn. The white man figures the Indian is some sort of wild animal, and all he cares about is killing the Indian out."

"Don't look like there's much chance for improvement,'' Cloud observed. ''Neither side has any inclination to do anything except fight.''

''In the long run it'll end the white man's way,'' Easter said. ''There aren't many Comanches—a few thousand, maybe. But there are more white men than there are blades of grass along the river. The Indian moves around from place to place. But where the white man goes, he stays. He takes the land, and he keeps it.'' Sadly she asked, ''What will become of my people then?''

Cloud had no answer. Hard for him to remember, sometimes, that in ways she was more Indian than white. He could sympathize with her concern, even though he couldn't see his way clear to agree with it. He had seen too many murdered men to have any particularly soft feeling toward the Indian.

''I'm like the others,'' he told her. ''I can't help but hate. Maybe I'm wrong—likely I oughtn't to be that way. But that's how it is, and I can't stop it. They hate us as much as we hate them. Who's to say which side is wrong?''

Trying to change the subject then, he said, ''It'd sure be worth a lot if somebody was to explore this country and map the waterin's.''

''You've been over quite a bit of the country now,'' she said. ''Maybe *you* could draw a map.''

''And show all the waterin' places I haven't found?''

''You'll find one. That spring I was telling you about, it's somewhere up ahead of us. I don't know how far; maybe a few hours, maybe another day. But it's there.''

''I ain't sure these horses have got another day. We've punished them somethin' awful.''

''We'll find it.''

They lay in silence awhile then. In the darkness Cloud could make out the shape of Easter Rutledge lying on her blanket, the curve of her hips, the gentle swell and fall of her breasts as she breathed. He knew he should turn away and sleep, but he couldn't. He kept staring at her, wishing things could have been different, wishing . . .

He sensed that she was looking at him, too. He heard her soft voice say, "Cloud?"

"What is it, Easter?"

A long pause, then she said, "Nothing, I guess. Good night."

He turned over, facing the other way. "Good night."

Next day was as bad as the last one had been. Even coffee didn't make the brackish water taste much better, although its color helped hide the mud. They broiled their bacon, sipped the foul coffee, then swung into their saddles and started out.

The sun beat down without mercy. Cloud didn't know just what day it was, but he knew the peak of summer should have passed. Soon, now, the smell of fall should be in the air. He rode with shoulders slumped, his eyes and mouth burning. His lips were dry and chapped, and when he tried to talk, it felt as if they were cracking. Easter rode much the same way, her head down, her slender shoulders pinched in. Glancing at her often, Cloud could see her tongue run over her dry lips, trying to wet them. But her tongue was dry, too.

He took his canteen from the saddlehorn and extended it to her. She shook her head. "Wait till I need it," she murmured.

It came to him then that he hadn't heard a word of complaint from her. White woman or not, the Indian training had made her strong as leather.

They stopped a while at noon out on the bald, open prairie. Strangely, the brackish water didn't taste bad at all anymore. Cloud didn't try to eat, for he feared that would make him even thirstier. He sat beside Easter in the shadow of the horses, resting. Even with the shade, the sun's heat rose up from the ground and wrapped itself around them like a stifling blanket. He looked down at the woman, marveling at the silence in which she had borne her misery.

This is a woman! he thought. *One in a thousand, and I'm lettin' her get away!*

He put his arm around her shoulder and said, "We'll make it, Easter."

She leaned to him, her head on his shoulder. "Cloud, I'm sorry I brought you to all this."

"If you'd known, would you have changed your mind about comin'?"

She shook her head. "No, but I'd have come alone. I wouldn't have told you and made you share it."

At midafternoon Cloud squinted into the shimmering heat waves on the horizon and reined up quickly. "Hold it, Easter," he exclaimed. "There's somethin' up yonder. Indians, maybe."

Before he could stop it, his horse raised its head, ears pointed forward, and nickered. From ahead came an answering nicker.

If it's Indians, Cloud thought with a stab of desperation, *our bread is dough!*

There was no need to run, for the horses couldn't have done it. Besides, there was nowhere to go. Cloud blinked, trying to clear his eyes.

"It's not Indians," he said at last, a thin whistle of relief passing between his cracked lips. "It's a bunch of mustangs, wild horses."

As they came closer, he watched them carefully. They were taking their time, pausing to graze. "They've already been to water," he said. "If they was just goin' to water they wouldn't be stoppin' along thisaway."

The mustangs broke into a run as the two riders neared

them. They warily circled far around and paused on a rise to look back.

"Easter, all we got to do now is backtrack them. It won't be far to water."

He rode with the rifle across his lap, for where there was a waterhole there might be Indians. He doubted that the mustangs would have watered had men been around, but he didn't want to ride in unprepared.

Ahead he could make out a grove of cottonwood trees, their leaves a welcome green against the brass of a hostile summer sky. From the way the horses picked up, Cloud knew they had smelled water. He felt his pulse quicken as they moved nearer the trees. His dry tongue touched parched lips, and all he could think of was a pool of clear, sweet water—deep and cool.

He held up his hand for Easter to stay back as he eased up to the water, hand tight on the rifle. He looked around, anxiously scanning the trees, the rim of the pool, the rolling prairie which stretched on beyond. Finally he nodded and said, "It's all right, Easter."

Cloud stepped down and loosened the cinches. He dropped the reins and let his horse drink. He reached up and helped Easter down.

"There's a spring right over yonder," he observed. "It'll be a little cleaner than drinkin' after the horses."

Easter replied, "I'm too thirsty to let the horses worry me." He took out the cups and dipped water from the spring, handing the first cup to Easter. He gulped down most of his without stopping for breath. For a moment a spell of weakness passed through him. Then a sigh escaped him, and he smiled.

"Never was nobody ever distilled a drink to match good, cool water."

Easter drank thirstily. Cloud was tempted to warn her to go slow, but he figured she knew. When her cup was empty, he took it and dipped it full for her again. "Just this one more," he said, "then we wait awhile. People have died from drinkin' too much water."

When they had finished for a while, Cloud led the horses away from the water and unsaddled them, staking them in the shade. They wanted more water, but he said, "Just you-all wait awhile, boys. You'll get back to it directly."

He walked around the pool, still feeling dry and wanting more water himself, but knowing he had to hold back. He found where the pool drained off at the far end into a creekbed that meandered out across the prairie, probably to disappear a few hundred yards away. He heard a footstep behind him and turned.

Easter said, "This is the place I told you about. We've camped here several times. From here on, I know my way."

Cloud nodded, sorrow drifting over him. "Then I expect you'll be wantin' to leave me now."

"It's too dangerous for you to come any farther. You've already come too far, I'm afraid."

"I wouldn't have done otherwise."

She nodded, her eyes level with his. "I know."

"I don't want to see you go, Easter."

She nodded again. "Some ways, I hate to go. But I have to, and you know I have to."

He took her hands. "You can't leave now. You're too tired, and your horse is too tired."

"We'll rest the night. We'll go in the morning." He felt the pressure of her hand. "You'll stay with me?"

"I'll stay."

Taking his rifle, he walked off down the creek out of sight. Then he set the rifle down within reach and took off his clothes. He eased into the creek and gave a long sigh as he slowly sank his body into the cool water. He sat where the creek was shallow, leaning back on his elbows with only his head out of water. There he sat a long time, soaking. There was a strange thing about going for a long time without water: the body seemed to sap itself of moisture, drying the skin, shrinking the man. Yet, when water was found, it did almost as much good to soak in the water as to drink it, for the body would absorb moisture like a sponge.

Cloud sat this way a long time, knowing Easter was doing the same up at the main pool, and not wanting to disturb her.

When at last he climbed out, most of his thirst was gone. He was fresher now, the weariness lifted from his shoulders. He tried whistling, but found his lips still a little dry for that.

When he had put his clothes on again, he walked on down the creek, looking for game. To his surprise, he came upon a small group of buffalo. Nearsighted, they had not seen him. He knelt in the protection of the brush and took careful aim on a fleshy young cow, leveling his sights on her lungs. From experience he knew that was the best place to hit a buffalo. Squeezing the trigger, he saw the dust puff as the bullet struck where he had aimed it. The cow's hind legs folded. She swayed on her forelegs a moment, slinging her head, then fell heavily on her side.

Shying away from the shot, the other buffalo trotted off, then turned to look back. In a moment they caught the smell of blood and broke into a run that left a fog of dust. When they were gone, Cloud walked out and slit the cow's throat. He waited for her to die, then cut away a hind quarter and threw it over his shoulder with the hide still on it. Back bent under the weight, he carried it to the spring.

Easter had already started a fire. Cloud said jokingly, "Behold, the mighty hunter brings meat to camp," somewhat as he had heard it bragged a couple of times in the camp of friendly Tonkawas.

He could tell by a quick frown of disapproval that she didn't appreciate it. She evidently thought he was making fun of Indian ways, and he knew he *had* been, a little.

She said, "I saw the buffalo run, and I knew you wouldn't miss."

He hung the hindquarter from a tree where Easter could slice it. While she set about fixing supper for them, he watered the horses again, then hobbled and staked them on the grass. The man and the woman ate silently, their eyes dwelling upon each other, and sadness in both.

By the time they had finished eating and putting the camp in order, it was dark. Cloud laid out his saddle and spread his blanket. He sat on it and stared off into the darkness, wrapped in thought. Easter watched him a while, then moved to him and sat down beside him.

"What're you thinking, Cloud?"

"Thinkin' I'll never see you again. It's a bitter thought, Easter."

Leaning to him, she said, "There'll be another woman, Cloud. Just keep looking and you'll find her."

He shook his head. "You're the one I want, Easter, the only one I've ever really wanted. Don't you have any of the same feeling for me, any of it atall?"

Easter's hand lifted slowly and rested on his shoulder. She turned her face up, her lips parted as if to speak. He touched her cheek and found it wet with a tear.

"Kiss me, Cloud," she whispered.

He pulled her close. Her lips were warm and eager, her hands pressing against his back. He held her that way a long time, crushing her as the powerful want boiled up in him like a thunderhead.

"Cloud," she whispered, "we won't think about tomorrow. Let's think only of now—of *us!*"

Eleven

CLOUD WAS THE FIRST TO LEAVE THE SPRING. RIDING south with the morning sun just breaking across the prairie, he paused a moment to look back. Over his shoulder he saw Easter sitting on her horse at the spring, watching him go. He lifted his hand, and she waved back at him. Then she turned her horse about and disappeared.

Cloud clenched his fist and felt his throat go tight again.

"Well, I tried," he murmured. "But a white woman is stubborn enough, and I guess a Comanche is worse."

He touched spurs to the horse and angled southeastward, toward the settlements. He tried to put his mind on other things, like the old days before the war when he ran his own cattle on open grass to the east—not easy times, but enjoyable times when a man had freedom. He thought of old friends he had known, many of them gone now to the battlefields of Virginia. He thought of the Texas

Mounted Rifles, of Aaron Barcroft and Quade Guffey and Miguel Soto.

But try though he did, he could not push Easter from his mind. Again and again she came back to him until he gave up and let her take over. He remembered how he had first seen her, running like a deer, turning on him in defiance. He remembered her as he had seen her that day she went into Brush Hill, bewildered, trying not to show her fright. He remembered his own awakening to the magic of her and wondering if she felt any of it for him. Most of all he remembered last night, when she had shown too late that she loved him just as he loved her.

Too late! Many a time in his life he had wanted something, or had thought he wanted it—a horse, cattle, land of his own. But now he knew he had never wanted anything before the way he wanted Easter Rutledge.

He rode with his head down, blind to everything but the sorrow in his heart.

After a long time he knew he had to think of other things. Easter Rutledge was in his past now. He had to forget her—or *try* to.

A movement on a rise made him snap to attention, grabbing instinctively at the rifle, jerking it half out of the scabbard before he realized that what he had seen was only a few antelope, running to get ahead of him. He watched them cut in front of him and cross over from his left to his right. *Wake up!* he told himself roughly. *Life ain't over, but it could be if you don't keep your eyes propped open. They could've been Indians just as easy as antelope.*

It came to him then that where there were antelope, water probably was not too far away. He hadn't given much consideration to water yet, for the canteen was full and the morning heat had not yet begun to make him thirst. But he realized how important it might be if he could find water up here, could remember it and make a decent enough rough map so that others might also find it. That spring back yonder was a good starting place. He knew the direction he had been riding and how long it had taken him to cover the ground. Now, if he could find the water. . . .

He watched the horizon, and he watched the ground at his horse's feet. He watched for wild-animal trails that might lead him to water, and finally he found one: an old buffalo trail. It hadn't been used in a long time. He couldn't be sure whether to go up it or down it. He took a chance and rode down it awhile. Presently another old trail cut in and joined it. Eventually the trail he followed joined another, which had been used recently by animals. He stopped to study the signs. Buffalo, antelope, a few horses.

The latter worried him. Mustangs, probably, but how could he know?

He came upon the seep unexpectedly and found himself alone there. No Indians. Relieved, he dismounted and loosened the cinch to let the horse drink. Now that he saw the water, Cloud felt thirsty himself. He knelt above the horse and drank as closely as he could to the point where the water seeped out. It had a tang of gyp that made him wrinkle his nose. But it was wet, and its taste was not nearly so bad as the mudhole he and Easter had found on the way up here.

Water like this was hard on men's bowels when they weren't used to it. Many a time Cloud had boiled a strong tea out of cottonwood bark to cure diarrhea. It wasn't the best medicine—it was almost as bad as the ailment—but it was often the only one to be had. Here there weren't even any cottonwoods.

He had been afraid either he or Easter would sicken on

the muddy water they had been forced to drink. Luckily they hadn't.

After that stuff, nothing can kill me now, he thought wryly.

Riding again, he thought how glad Aaron Barcroft would be to get his hands on a map that would guide him to the waterholes and lead him up onto the open prairie of the lower plains.

But, came a chilling thought, *he'll probably be even gladder to get his hands on me!*

Up to now Cloud had not given much consideration to the captain. There had been Easter to worry about, her problem to be solved. Purposely Cloud had shoved aside any thought of what the captain might do. Now he could no longer ignore Barcroft.

At best, he'll court-martial me. At worst, he'll hang me!

He felt of his throat, and gooseflesh rose on his skin. Damn! The man just might do it. Fact of the matter, he was more likely to than not.

He's got a back stiff as a poker, Cloud thought. *He's not much given to compromise when he believes he's in the right. He took a woman's baby from her when he thought it was the proper thing to do. He's been through enough hell of his own that no matter what the other man might be tangling with, it looks tame to the captain.*

So, he considered, *if I ride back there now, it'll be my neck.*

Desertion, Barcroft would call it. And delivering a white woman into the hands of the Indians.

Lord, how could I expect him to figure it otherwise?

Maybe the Lawtons could talk to him. Cloud pondered that, then shook his head. Nobody'd ever been able to tell him much. Cloud had seen the captain really unbend only once, when he rigged the escape of the young conscription-dodgers after one of them saved his life. And that had been a weak moment. Later, given time to think, he might not have done it.

If I'm smart, I'll just keep right on riding. I won't stop for Barcroft or anybody.

A man could ride south into Mexico and just sit there till the war was over. Lots of them were doing it. He might have to be a little careful about meeting people on the way down—might even have to tell some outrageous lies.

Bet a feller could make himself a living out of cattle or something down in Mexico and have something to bring out with him when the war was over.

He had heard there was a little trouble down in Mexico, too; some kind of ruckus with a bunch of Frenchmen. He wondered what business a Frenchman had in Mexico anyway. But no matter, an American could stay clear of that if he tried.

Mexico! Man, that was a long way to go—a long way from Easter Rutledge. But what difference would it make, when he could never see her again anyway? Wouldn't matter if he went twenty miles or a thousand, she was lost to him. Maybe she would be easier to put out of mind if he knew she was far away.

Well, sir, that was the thing to do—head south and not stop till he pulled up to dry the muddy water off of him on the far side of the Rio Grande.

But a worry tugged at him. Conscience first, for he would be leaving the frontier service at a time when it desperately needed men. Still, he would rather leave it this way than at the end of Barcroft's hang rope. Second, there was the idea that any knowledge he might gain of the waterholes, the plains route, would be lost with him if he left. No telling what it might be worth to somebody else to know what Cloud was finding out up here on the lower edge of the high plains.

Well, there was one way to fix it. He'd go by Lige Moseley's and draw a map. He'd let Moseley pass it on later, when Cloud had time to get far enough south so that he no longer had to worry about pursuit.

Badly as Aaron Barcroft might hate Cloud after this, he would be glad to get the map. And he wouldn't be ashamed to use it.

Maybe if I leave them this much, the rest of the bunch won't think too bad of me.

It took longer to get back than it had taken to ride out, for Cloud and Easter had been pushing hard at first. With little to go on but instinct, but with full faith in that, Cloud headed as straight for Moseley's as he knew how. He made a dry camp, then found another waterhole. It was muddy, and he could almost smell the gyp in it. He didn't drink any of it, but in a tight place he could have. So could anyone else.

Not far from Moseley's, he came across the tracks. His heart jumped as he stepped down for a look. Plenty of them—riders and loose horses—headed northwest. And from droppings he could tell the trail was not more than a few hours old—perhaps as little as one or two.

The short hair lifted at the back of his neck. Indians! It wasn't that he had any real way of knowing, but a man developed an instinct for it sometimes, like a dog. He wondered how he had been lucky enough to miss them, for their trail was almost parallel to his. There was just enough divergence that somewhere back yonder they had passed one another, unbeknown.

He thought then of Lige Moseley. If these Indians hadn't changed direction, they had come right by his place. A worry built in him, putting a burning knot in the pit of his stomach. This wasn't any little raiding party. This had been a large band of warriors, enough of them to accomplish just about anything they set their minds to.

He spurred into an easy lope. He backtrailed the Indians, watching all the while for sign of captives or white victims along the way. At length he came upon a dead horse and stopped for a look. Moseley's brand! A chill passed through Cloud. He swung back into the saddle and spurred again, no longer sparing his horse.

A spot of color ahead of him caught his eye. Even before he got there, he knew what it was. His horse shied away as wind caught in the cloth of a skirt and rippled it gently. Heartsick, Cloud stepped to the ground and walked up to the still form of the girl, lying limp in the grass, arrows bristling from her breast. Choking, he knelt a moment with hat in his hand, his eyes burning with tears.

Samantha!

He swayed, the shock hitting him in the stomach like the kick of a mule. He remembered Samantha as he had seen her before, her pretty eyes filled with curiosity—with a vague longing—as she watched him, her long blonde hair hanging about her shoulders.

Somewhere up yonder a Comanche brave carried that hair now as a trophy.

Cloud found himself murmuring a prayer. Then he looked about for something to cover her body. Finding nothing, he took the slicker from behind his saddle and used that.

"I'll be back, girl," he said.

He rode on, his heart heavy as lead, for he knew what he must find now at Moseley's. He rode into the clearing and saw the vague drift of smoke being carried southward by the wind. The cabin was only half burned, for the Indians had not done a good job of setting the fire. In the grass around the house Cloud could see several patches of blood.

"They didn't take you easy, old-timer," he breathed.

He found Lige Moseley—what was left of him—beside

the corral fence, his body riddled with bullets, cruelly hacked and slashed.

They hated him, Cloud knew. They took it out on him this time.

Mouth drawn tight, Cloud walked on to the cabin. In the front yard by the door lay the oldest boy, Luke. Mrs. Moseley lay in the doorway. Carefully Cloud stepped over her and walked inside the smouldering cabin. In a moment he was out again, retching.

The Indians hadn't missed a thing. Moseley's escape tunnel had not helped his family this time.

Blinded, Cloud leaned against the wall of the cabin and buried his burning eyes in his arms. He clenched and unclenched his fists, praying one moment, cursing the next. Finally he sat down heavily upon the ground, shaking his head and swallowing the huge lump that choked him.

"Lige, Lige . . . what an awful price to pay!"

He wondered then how many others had paid this price for the right to try to build a home, the right to move out and claim a raw land and try to make it grow. How many had died on this one raid?

"Lige," he spoke then, looking toward the still body of the old man, "I was fixin' to run off to Mexico. Fixin' to run off like a cur dog and let you-all do your own fightin'. Shameful thing for a man to figure on, ain't it?" His face twisted. "Well, I ain't goin' to do it now. Somebody's got a lot to pay for, and I'll do my best to collect it, I promise you that!"

He got to his feet then, fists tight, color high in his face. "I swear to God, Lige, I'll stay here and fight!"

It occurred to him that he had not tried to account for all of the Moseley children. He had taken one look, then had fled. Now, he knew, he had to go back and take count, to be sure whether all were dead, or if possibly some were missing. He forced himself to the door. There he hesitated a moment, stiffened his back and went in.

Presently he was out again, face gray and sick. One missing, the little girl named Joanna. Two years old, she was—maybe three. Cloud was certain he hadn't overlooked her body on the trail, and it was not here. He searched around the cabin afoot, around the clearing.

They had taken her prisoner, then. It didn't seem likely, the way they had butchered the rest of the family, but there could be no other explanation. The Comanches were like that sometimes. Maybe one of the warriors had taken a fancy to the little girl's looks. Maybe she had tried to fight them, and they had liked her spirit. They often honored those who fought hardest against them. Whatever the reason, she was with them. She *had* to be.

"Lige," he said, "it'd be better if she was dead. But I'll find her if I can. I'll go after her by myself and steal her back if there's any possible way to do it."

And if he couldn't get her back? He knew the grim answer to that. He'd kill her, even though it meant his own death.

He looked around the ruins of the cabin for anything he might take along in the way of supplies—food, powder, lead. But the Indians hadn't overlooked much. What they hadn't taken, they had slashed to ribbons, spilled or poured out. Even the Moseley's old family Bible had been ripped apart. Cloud found the binding lying on the dirt floor, with a few of the loose pages scattered around. Indians often took all the books they could find. They used the paper to stuff inside their bull-hide shields, for they had discovered that tightly packed paper would sometimes stop a bullet.

Cloud picked up one of the Bible pages the fire hadn't singed. It was the Moseley family record, the birthdates of the children carefully written with goosequill and ink, and the dates of a couple of their deaths, noted afterward.

The tears came back to Cloud as he looked at this record. He could write the rest of it now, if it would mean anything. But it wouldn't. Carefully he folded the page and put it in his pocket. Someday, perhaps, he would come back and put up a monument of some kind.

He looked around him a last time. All this, gone for nothing. All these lives thrown away, with little left to mark their passing except these names written so carefully in an old family Bible.

He stepped outside and walked to his horse. "Well, old friend, looks like we've got all that ride to do over again. It may kill us both, but we'll do it."

He put his foot into the stirrup and lifted himself into the saddle again. He was about to pull the horse around and head him northward when he heard the sound of hoofs and saw the riders break out of the timber and move toward him in a long trot.

In front rode Miguel Soto. And just behind him, Aaron Barcroft.

Twelve

CAPTAIN BARCROFT GRAVELY RODE UP TO CLOUD, his eyes like flint. "Cloud, I never expected to see you here. In fact, I never thought I'd see you again anywhere."

Uneasily Cloud said, "I reckon not, sir."

Barcroft held out his hand. "You're under arrest, you know. I'll take your gun."

Cloud reached for it, then hesitated. "You can have it if you really want it, Captain. But don't you reckon you'll need all the guns you can get?"

The captain lowered his hand, his eyes probing at Cloud. "That's the truth, I will. I'll want your word—"

"I'll promise you anything you ask for, Captain," Cloud said earnestly. "When this is over you can have my guns, do what you want to with me, and I won't whimper none. But right now I want to take part in whatever the Rifles do about this." He made a motion with his hand, toward the ruins of the Moseley home. "I owe it to Lige."

Barcroft shrugged. "I can't spare anybody to take you back to the settlement, and I know there are enough Unionists in the outfit see that you got a gun anyway, if you wanted one. So you keep yours, Cloud, for now. Later . . . we'll see." He turned to look over the carnage. His eyes pinched half shut. Cloud saw the man's jaw ridge. Barcroft asked huskily, "All of them dead?"

Cloud nodded. "All that's here. The oldest girl, I found her a ways up the trail—dead. There's a little girl missin'. I reckon them Indians took her along."

"How old a girl?"

"Three, or thereabouts."

Barcroft said, almost in a whisper, "Three . . . like mine." His hand knotted on the saddlehorn. "I told Moseley," he gritted. "He wouldn't listen." He looked down, face saddened. "They tried to tell *me* once, and *I* wouldn't listen. You're a frontiersman, Cloud, so you ought to know. What makes a man do it? Why does he stay when the odds are so heavy against him?"

Cloud shook his head. "I can't rightly say, Captain. All I know is, if it wasn't for men like Lige—and families like his—we'd still be sittin' around Plymouth Rock, afraid to go out in the woods."

The captain nodded grimly. "You've said what's true. All civilization is built over the bones of men like Moseley."

Cloud said, "Lige believed the Lord intended for white men to have this country. He told me once it was like when God sent the children of Israel into the land of Canaan. Some would die, but the most would make it. Maybe Lige was right; maybe the Lord intended it that way. Maybe He gives men like Lige a divine call, the way He does a preacher."

The men who had come with Barcroft were scattered about inspecting the ruins. The shock of what they saw held their voices down almost to a whisper and splotched their faces an angry red. There were more men than Cloud had seen ride with the captain before. Most of the regular Rifles were there, as well as a dozen or more civilian volunteers. They led packhorses, well provisioned.

Came ready this time, Cloud thought. *Captain must figure to stay on the trail however long it takes to get the job done.*

The men began gathering around the captain again. Cloud could sense a grim, smoldering anger in them. They sat their horses or stood on the ground, watching the captain expectantly, impatient to be on the move.

Barcroft picked out a couple of youngsters from among the volunteers, boys still in their late teens. He said, "Lads, I've got a job for you. We can't just leave these poor people this way. They deserve a decent burial. You'd do me a great service if you'd volunteer to stay here and give them one." When the boys showed hesitancy, he added, "It won't be an easy job. It'll take all the manhood you can muster. Will you do it?"

Approached that way, the boys could do little but consent.

Cloud said, "Captain, we ought to get the boys to go along with us a ways and fetch back Samantha Moseley. We can't just leave her out there."

The captain nodded. He turned then to the men who gathered around him. "Men," he said in as grave a voice as Cloud had ever heard him use, "here you see the nature of our enemy. You see why, this time and every time, we need to follow him till we catch him, no matter how hard it is, no matter how long it takes. We need to show him we're prepared to answer his savagery with a bloody vengeance. This may be a long, hard ride with an awful fight at the end of it. It could be a costly fight that some of us won't come home from. But this I swear to you: we won't turn back till we've gotten it done. If there's anyone here who doesn't feel he can stay all the way, I want him to leave us right now."

He looked about him at the hard-set faces. No one spoke or moved. Satisfied, he said, "I thought that's how it would be. I've never been one to brag on men, but I'm proud of you. You're all sure now? From the time we leave here there'll be no turning back. If you ride away from here with me, you've committed yourselves to stay until it's finished."

Some men nodded, some just held still. But none pulled back. "All right, then," said the captain, "we'll water our horses, then we'll ride." He turned for a glance at Cloud. "Your horse worn out?"

"He's been a long ways, sir. Reckon if he had to, he'd go some more."

"Swap with one of the boys on the burial detail. Their horses are fresher. I'm not going to leave you anywhere along the way, Cloud."

"I have no intention of *bein'* left, sir!"

He moved his saddle to one of the boys' horses and pulled in beside the other men. Seward Prince, who had fought with him over the Union, just gave him a quick glance of dislike. Quade Guffey shook Cloud's hand gravely, knowing how Cloud felt about the Moseleys.

Barcroft said, "Cloud, you'd just as well take the lead with Miguel."

"You mean you'd trust me up there, Captain?"

The captain grunted. "Rather have you up there where I can watch you."

They strung out across the prairie, following the clear trail the Indians had beaten into the sod with their stolen horses. They came to the body of the girl. The men dismounted silently to stand with hats in their hands. A gray-haired rider who was a part-time preacher bowed his head and spoke a prayer that started with a quiet plea for mercy upon the innocent soul of the girl and ended in an impassioned promise of bloody vengeance.

"She was Thy child, Lord," he declared, his angry face lifting to the summer sky, "and the hand of the heathen smote her down. But Thou shalt have Thy vengeance! Deliver the heathen into our hands, O Lord, and we will be Thy messengers of judgment!"

Cloud held himself apart from the others. His eyes were squeezed shut, but he could still see the girl in his mind.

Miguel Soto moved over to him and spoke with sympathy, "She was a most pretty girl."

Conscience-stricken, Cloud only nodded. He couldn't speak.

She was in love with me, or she thought she was. And all I felt was embarrassment. I wish it could have been different. She deserved a better man than me. She deserved a better fate than this.

Riding away, the captain pulled up beside Cloud. "That's what they did to one woman. Yet you turned another one over to the Indians."

Cloud didn't feel like arguing with the captain. He didn't feel like talking at all. "It wasn't the same with Easter, sir; you know that. Besides, I didn't turn her over to the Indians. She turned herself over."

"You took her there."

"It wasn't my choice. I couldn't stop her; she was goin' anyway. I wanted to see she got there alive."

"How far did you go?"

"A good ways up yonder, sir."

"Up on those plains? There's no water up there."

"There's water, sir, if you can find it. It's scarce, and a lot of it's bad. But it's there."

"Could you find that water again?"

Cloud tapped his forehead. "I made maps up here, sir. I could find it."

The captain chewed his lip a minute, eyes squinting into the northwest. They were calculating eyes, and Cloud could see hope growing in them. At length he turned again to Cloud. "What you did was a hanging offense. Any court-martial would call it desertion in time of war. If I'd found you at another time, another place, I'd have conducted a drumhead court-martial and hanged you in twenty minutes.

"But now, after what we saw at Moseley's, and that girl back there, what you did doesn't seem important at all anymore. Maybe we'll even be able to use some of the knowledge you gained. No telling what we may need to know before we get through this trip."

They rode without stopping until it was too dark to follow the tracks. The captain ordered a dry camp with no fires. No picket lines were set up for the horses. Each man slept with his horse staked close by him, ready to ride in a moment. Barcroft posted a heavy guard, half expecting the Indians to double back and try for the pursuers' horses. It had happened before.

But the Comanches didn't come that night. Next morning the Texans came across the camp where they had halted to rest, pushing on with dawn.

"Bound to know they're bein' followed," Cloud observed to Miguel Soto.

Soto said, "Somebody always follow them this far. But not many times anybody he ever go much farther than this. Most times, we have to turn back when we get about here."

Miguel added grimly, "I wish now when I live with the Comanche we come this way just one time. Then maybeso I could take the company there—all the way!"

All that day they followed the trail. It began to meander a little, then abruptly straightened again.

Cloud said to Miguel, "They probably figured there wasn't anybody after them anymore and they got careless awhile. Then one of them scouted back and saw us. They sure yanked up the slack."

The riders pushed their horses all they dared. It was hard to resist spurring into a hard run and trying to catch up all at once. But every man knew how futile that would be, how disastrous to the horses.

Dusk caught them, and it was difficult to tell whether they had actually made much gain on the Indians or not. Weariness had settled over the men. They didn't talk as they rode. They just sat slump-shouldered in the saddles and moved doggedly on, hating the colors of fading sunset because this meant they soon had to give up the trail until tomorrow.

Barcroft held up his hand and stopped the men. "We'll hold here a little while. We all need coffee, I expect, so we'll stop early enough that we can afford to build fires. Hurry it up. We'll need to put the fires out again before it turns full dark. Then we'll ride on a little way farther before we camp."

Cloud didn't know how tired he really was until he stepped down and felt his knees buckle. He almost fell.

Soto grinned sympathetically. He appeared to be holding up better. Funny, thought Cloud, how a Mexican so often seemed to have more stamina, always seemed born to the saddle.

"Cloud, my frien'," said Soto, "you got any coffee?"

Cloud shook his head. "Haven't hardly got anything, except an appetite."

Miguel said, "I got plenty. You and me, we share together."

"Poor trade for you. About all I can give you is gratitude."

"That," said Miguel, "is plenty much."

Engrossed in their coffee, their slim supper, the chance for a few moments of rest, the weary men lost their watchfulness. Barcroft had not posted guard because he didn't intend to be there long and expected no counterattack. If the Indians came for horses, he had reasoned, they probably would do so after dark.

Therefore the raiding party was almost upon them before anyone saw it. Someone shouted the alarm as the Indians suddenly showed up on a rise and came riding as hard as their horses would run.

The first thought of every man was to grab his own mount and keep the Comanches from getting it. Men jumped away from the fires, spilling coffee, hurling food aside as they grabbed at bridle reins. In seconds the Texas line bristled with guns. But the dozen or so Comanches didn't try to strike the whole line. They knifed down toward a thin end of it, arrows streaking, guns aflame. Outflanked, most of the Rifles were unable to return effective fire for fear of hitting their own men.

At the very end of the line with Miguel Soto, Cloud grabbed his horse, then dropped to one knee and began to fire at the swift Indian party. He saw Barcroft's lieutenant, Elkin, go down with an arrow in him. He saw Captain Barcroft run to the man's side, then pitch forward, hand to his chest.

An Indian whirled around to stab at the captain with a lance. Cloud brought his pistol up and fired. The lance tipped and drove into the ground. The Indian was hurled off his horse by the powerful leverage of it. Jumping to his feet, Cloud let his horse go and sprinted to the captain's side, pausing to fire again as the downed Indian struggled to his feet. The Comanche went down to stay.

Another Indian drove at them, but Cloud fired on him and forced him to pull away. He knelt by the captain's side, the smoking pistol in his hand, his anxious eyes peering through the smoke for signs of another threat.

As suddenly as they had come, the Indians were gone. The smoke drifted away and the dust settled. Cloud turned the captain over and saw the spreading stain on the man's dusty shirt. He ripped the shirt away to get at the wound. The captain gritted his teeth.

"How many dead, Cloud?" he wanted to know. "How many?"

"Don't know yet, sir. You just lay still."

"Dammit, find out how many!"

"Captain, you ain't in no shape to be worryin' yourself about it one way or the other."

He saw Miguel Soto walking up with Cloud's horse. "Thanks, Miguel," he said. "Figured I'd lost him."

"*Por nada,*" shrugged the Mexican. "I share with you my coffee, but I don' share with you my horse."

Cloud found the captain's wound to be low in the shoulder. "Close, Captain," he said. "A little lower and it'd have been in the heart."

"Well," the captain breathed tightly, "it wasn't, so let me up. I've got to see about the company."

Cloud shook his head. "Captain, the company's goin' to have to do without you, or else turn back. You've gone as far as you can go."

The doctor, Walt Johnson, showed up with his bag. He glanced in dismay at the captain, then forced a thin smile. "They told me you were dead, Captain. No such luck, eh?"

"Patch me up so I can ride!"

"Shape you're in, Captain," Johnson said, "you'd be lucky to ride in a wagon."

"We have no wagon."

"Sort of narrows it down, doesn't it, sir?"

The captain seemed to give up then. He sank back, hopelessness in his eyes. "Damn them, what were they after? They knew they couldn't whip us all. What did they come for?"

Cloud said, "Fun, maybe. Thought they'd hit us a lick and get the hell out. And they probably figured they could get away with some of the horses, too. Been spyin' on us a spell, more'n likely. Seen us stop for supper and thought they'd bust in and run off all the horses they could. Leave enough of us afoot and there'd be nothin' left but for all of us to turn back."

"Did they get many horses?"

"No, sir, not hardly a one."

"And men . . . I asked you once about men."

"Just one dead that I've seen, sir."

Barcroft's face fell. "Elkin?"

Cloud nodded. "Yes, sir, Elkin. Way he went down, I don't reckon he hardly felt a thing."

Barcroft shut his eyes against a surge of pain that stiffened him hard as a rock. When it passed, he opened his eyes again. They were glazed now. He spoke tightly: "Elkin . . . best man I had. Always figured if anything happened to me . . . he'd be the one to take over."

The doctor broke in, "Captain, that bullet's got to come out, and pretty soon. Longer we wait, the worse it'll be."

Barcroft whispered, "Get on with it, then."

The doctor warned, "It'll hurt pretty bad. I've got some whiskey along—brought it for just such an emergency. Drink enough of that and maybe it won't seem quite as bad."

"No whiskey," Barcroft said flatly. "I can't be drunk and command."

"You can't command now anyway," said the doctor.

He glanced at Cloud. "Get me some hot water started, will you?"

The doctor went after the whiskey, and Cloud got some water on to boil over a fire. The doctor brought the bottle and handed it to Barcroft. "I'm the doctor," he said firmly, "and I'm telling you to drink it!"

The captain took a long pull at the bottle and swore at the fire of it. "Where'd you get this?"

"Just drink it . . . sir!"

Even with the whiskey, the captain fainted before they got the bullet out. He spent a restless night, tossing in fever. By morning, though, the fever had subsided to some extent. The captain's eyes seemed to be sunk far back into dark hollows. He tried to sit up, but he couldn't make it.

The doctor told him, "You've got to go back, sir, there's no alternative."

Barcroft said in a thin, fevered voice, "I vowed we wouldn't stop this time. I promised to follow the Indians all the way."

"The company might be able to go on, but *you* can't."

The captain's pain-ridden eyes studied the worried men gathered around him. At length his gaze settled on Cloud.

"Cloud," he said, "Likely as not those Indians'd throw you off the trail sooner or later, and you'd have to go by instinct. Could you find the watering places you told me about?"

Cloud frowned and looked at the other men. "I think I could, sir."

"Thinking isn't enough. You'll *have* to do it."

Cloud shrugged. "All right, sir, I *will* find them."

"Have you ever led men? Commanded them, I mean?"

"Never no bunch like this."

"You'll have to do it now. I'm turning the company over to you!"

Cloud rocked back on his heels. "*Me,* Captain?" He took a deep breath. "Why *me?*"

"It's not that I want to, Cloud. If I had a choice, any choice at all . . ." He scowled. "I've watched you. Unionist or not, you know what you're doing, and you've got an advantage over everyone else here. You've been up into the edge of the high country where these Indians are heading. It just seems to fall into your lap, doesn't it?"

"Captain," Cloud pleaded, "why don't you turn it over to somebody else? Just let me be a guide—a scout—like I've always been. I never figured to be no officer, never had no trainin' thataway."

"You know what you need for *this* job, probably better than any man here. It hurts me worse than it does you, just having to give it to you. So take it and go on. That's an order!"

Cloud rubbed the back of his neck, still unable to accept what had happened to him. "Captain, I don't know much about the military, but I thought I was under arrest. You sure don't turn a command over to a man who's under arrest."

Barcroft scowled again. "Then you're not under arrest anymore. You forget about it and I'll try to."

Cloud looked around him, worriedly studying the faces of the men, wondering how they would accept him, especially those strongly Confederate. "Boys," he said, "I don't really want this job, and if you-all don't want to follow me, I won't take it. It's up to you."

The captain protested, "It's not up to them. *I* gave the order."

Miguel Soto grinned thinly and nodded. Red-haired Quade Guffey said, "All right, new captain, you just tell us where you want us to go to."

Cloud looked at Seward Prince, the staunch Confederate. Prince frowned and dug his toe into the ground. He finally said, "This ain't no time to be fightin' over politics. Them Indians don't know one side from the other. Later, maybe, I'll fight you to hell and gone. But right now I'll follow you."

Cloud expected some vocal opposition, for he could see it in a few of the faces. But when Prince accepted him, the rest of the opposition seemed to dissolve.

"Just lead out," somebody spoke, "and let's go."

Cloud couldn't just ride off and leave the captain alone. He had a couple of men who had received slight wounds in the sudden raid last night. These he detailed to take the captain home. An hour's ride back, he had seen a grove of trees late the day before. He told the men to go there and cut a couple of long ones, then make a travois to carry the captain home.

As Cloud started to leave, the captain waved him over. "Cloud," he said, "the main thing now is to try to get that little girl back. I don't expect I'll ever find mine anymore. But get *this* one!"

Cloud promised, "We'll sure try, sir."

Thirteen

THEY FOUND WHERE THE INDIANS HAD STOPPED TO rest briefly during the night. On the run, Indians seldom rested any more than they had to. From this point, the single trail splintered into half a dozen.

Cloud cursed under his breath and said to Miguel Soto, "Been afraid all along they'd do this. When they couldn't run our horses off, they figured to get rid of us by splittin' up. We can't follow them all."

Quade Guffey suggested, "We could split up ourselves."

Cloud shook his head. "Mighty little I know about soldierin', but one thing I *do* know is that you don't want to divide your forces. We'll just have to pick one trail and stay with it." He turned to Miguel. "Reckon they'll all meet again farther along?"

Miguel said, "Sometimes they do. Not every time. With Comanche, is nothing ever sure."

Quade asked, "How we goin' to know which trail to stay with?"

"We don't. Just shut your eyes and pick one."

Quade took one that appeared most nearly to follow in the same direction as they had been riding. It was the one Cloud would have chosen.

They followed the trail an hour or so before this one split, too.

"Indians," Guffey growled. "They'll wear you to a nub, just makin' decisions."

Cloud gritted his teeth. Anybody could follow a hundred horses moving in a bunch. But it might not be easy to follow three or four ridden by men who knew how to hide their trail.

The late-summer sun built to a deadening heat as the riders moved along, the main body of horsemen staying to one side of the trail to prevent obliterating it in case Miguel and Cloud lost it and had to do some backtracking. They jogged in silence across this open, rolling prairie of brown grass that stretched on to infinity, fading from sight in waves of heat that writhed in ceaseless torment on the vague, brassy horizon.

As the day wore on, Cloud found himself looking back often at the men. He saw their shoulders begin to droop. He saw some of them turning for a wistful look over the back trail. At times the trail was so dim that the men had to ride along in a slow walk while Cloud and Miguel bent in the saddle, straining for sight of something to go by. Now and again they had to halt altogether and circle back for another try, picking up the trail somewhere behind and following it again, careful lest they lose it once more.

Finally, late in the day, the trail played out altogether. Miguel tried hard to pick it up, even got on his hands and knees and probed with his fingers at what he thought might be a horse track. It wasn't.

Until dark they hunted, but the Indians had covered the trail too well. Cloud felt a momentary wave of despair. "Led us right out to the thin edge of nothin' and then dropped us off."

He signaled the men to stop and fix supper. Sharing a fire with Miguel and Quade Guffey, he morosely stared into his coffee cup.

Guffey said, "No use blamin' yourself. Wouldn't have been any different if the captain had been in charge."

"Wasn't blamin' myself, or anybody. Just wonderin' which way to jump next."

"Don't look like we got much choice. We lost them. We'd just as well head home."

Cloud frowned. "Maybe we could find them again." To Guffey's questioning glance, he said, "I got a hunch where them Comanches might be headed. I been thinkin' about just goin' there ourselves, as fast as we can."

Guffey and Miguel straightened with interest. Guffey asked, "Where's that?"

"A spring Easter showed me. Best, she said, anywhere down on this part of the plains. Said the Indians use it a lot as a jumpin'-off place when they sashay south to plunder, and they meet there sometimes when they come back after a raid."

Guffey pointed out, "You don't know that they'll use it *this* time. That bunch we followed when we rescued her—*they* didn't meet on no spring. Why don't we go back to the place where we first found her?"

"They know *we* know where it's at. They *don't* know we know where the spring is."

Some of the men had begun to gather around and listen. Finally Seward Prince spoke up: "Cloud, how far is it to that spring?"

"Can't rightly say. It's a far piece yet."

"How do you know you can find it? You don't even know how far it is."

Chewing his lip, Cloud said, "I can find it, that's all. I've always had a good sense of direction. Ever I'm at a place, I can find my way back to it. Kind of an instinct, I guess."

"You feel sure of yourself, but how can we be sure of *you*?"

Cloud sought an answer but didn't find it. "The Lord gave me an instinct, and I've got faith in it. You'll just have to have faith too."

Prince grumbled, "I got faith in what I can see—a good horse, a gun. I ain't keen on somethin' I *can't* see, like somebody else's instinct."

Guffey stood up and heatedly faced the man. "You got somethin' better?"

Cloud held up his hand to stop the argument. "Boys, ain't no use us gettin' in an argument over this thing. I'm not takin' anybody someplace where he don't want to go." He stood up and looked around. By this time all the men were close enough to hear him. He drained the coffee cup and dropped it.

To all of them he said, "I'm not Captain Barcroft, and I won't even try to act like him. I got a proposition to make you. Them that don't want to go with me can turn around and head home, and no hard feelin's. Them that does choose to stick with me, I want them to know what the odds are. We've lost the trail. Chances aren't good that we'll pick it up again. Ahead of us, way off yonder, is a spring where I think the Comanches may be figurin' to meet up with one another. I can't guarantee to find it, but I *think* I can. And even if we find the spring, we can't be plumb sure that's where they're headed this time. All we can do is rely on the odds. And the odds are, that's where they'll go.

"Another thing: we know the Indians left a rear guard to spy on us last night. That's why they hit the camp the way they did. Now, they may still be out yonder watchin' us, seein' which way we're goin' to go. So if we do cut out across this prairie and head straight toward the spring, I think we ought to start in the night. With a little luck, we can be a long ways before any spies they've left catch on. That way, we'd be in better shape to surprise the bunch when we do find them."

Dr. Johnson said, "Sounds reasonable to me. If the captain had enough confidence to leave you in charge, I'll go with you."

Other men agreed with the doctor. In a minute almost no one was left except Seward Prince. Cloud stared levelly at him. "How about it, Prince?"

Prince looked around him and saw how the temper of the others seemed to be. He shrugged his heavy shoulders and said, "Well, it's a cinch I don't care none about goin' back by myself. I ain't got your instinct, Cloud; I'm *already* lost. So it looks like I got no choice."

Cloud warned him, "If you go, you'll take orders like everybody."

"I'll take orders. I'm liable to whip you later, but right now I'll take orders."

Cloud nodded in satisfaction. "Fair enough. Whip me later, if you can. Right now we better try to get a little rest. After a while we'll get up and head out in the dark." He paused and added, "And this time we'll do what we came for, boys. I can feel it in my bones."

They rode in starlight. It was barely bright enough to see each other and not become separated in the night. Cloud felt the weariness weighing in his own body and could see it in the sag of the other men. They hadn't rested long enough. Before long they would feel the horses giving out too.

They jogged along in silence, no one talking lest voices carry. They denied themselves the comfort of smoking tobacco, lest the glow be seen from afar. Some men who normally smoked were chewing their tobacco now, trying to defeat the craving that gnawed at them.

Cloud picked a course by the stars and followed it arrow-straight across the gentle roll of the dark prairie. He listened to the muffled thump of hoofbeats in the blackness behind him and was reassured. He knew he was riding across land he had never seen before, land east of the route he had ridden with Easter. Yet within him burned a certainty that he knew how to reach the spring. It was an instinct which came to many frontiersmen who spent their lives in a land beyond trails, beyond civilization. He never questioned the source of it. His faith was simple. As he saw it, the Lord put the instinct in a man with the intention that he use it. Either the man believed in it or he didn't. Cloud believed in it.

After long hours the sun came up, breaking across the right shoulders of the men. There had been no visible change in the prairie. The land over which their long shadows lanced in the golden glow of dawn was the same as they had seen at sundown, the same as they had ridden across all day yesterday. There seemed to be no end to this open land. Its unbroken sweep stretched out all around them, even seemed to move along with them, boundless as the rolling sea. Just grass—the short brown grass of the buffalo range—as far as man's vision reached.

Riding in moody silence, Cloud could not help wondering if eternity itself might not be like this, like a great endless plain of grass stretching on and on, a plain upon which a man might ride and search forever and never find a way to leave it.

He shook his head and tried to put his mind on something else. Just sleepy, he thought, and tired. *Letting my imagination run away. Got to keep my mind on my business.*

All day they rode like this. Occasionally Cloud stopped for a glance over the back trail, as if he expected to find Indians following them. He knew he wouldn't see any, even if they were there. Yet he couldn't keep from looking—looking and wondering.

By midafternoon he could see worry nagging at the men, too. He could feel dust-burned eyes turned upon him, could sense the doubt that began to build in the riders. Tired now, and thirsty, their canteens light because most of the water was gone, they were beginning to wonder if Cloud had led them astray.

The strain began to tell upon Cloud, too. It wasn't that he doubted himself, for he did not. He felt sure the spring lay somewhere ahead, and that he could find it. But he was afraid the men might give up—might turn against him before they reached it.

What would he do if they did? He knew what Captain Barcroft would have done—draw a gun and force them on. But Cloud could never do that. It wasn't his way. From behind him he began to hear grumbling. It wasn't general yet. It was scattered among the same men who always grumbled first. But like rottenness in a barrel of apples, it could soon spread.

The voice he feared most was that of Seward Prince, for he knew there were many who would follow Prince in whatever the man decided to do.

And at last, late in the day, he heard that voice.

"Well, Cloud, how about it? You still sure that instinct is workin'?"

Cloud turned, his face as calm as he could force it. "You haven't seen me alter my course any."

The answer was not one Cloud expected to hear. Prince said, "Then just keep a-ridin'. We'll stay with you."

After that, the grumbling quieted. Cloud felt a gratitude to the big rebel, and at the same time a wonder. If there was to be trouble, he had fully expected it to originate with Prince.

The buffalo trails were the first sign of water. Somehow, sight of it lifted Cloud's shoulders, and he wasn't so weary anymore. It had the same effect upon the men. They followed one of the trails awhile, and the horses began to get the scent of water.

Warily the men balanced rifles and shotguns across their saddles, ready in case there should be Indians at the waterhole. But they found the place clear. Cloud looked it over a moment, and his spirits soared.

"I know this place," he said to Miguel Soto. "I was here." He turned back to the men. "Boys, I'd go kind of sparin' on this water. It's all right in small doses, but too much of it'll sure bust the puckerstring."

This wasn't the spring he sought. It was the somewhat gyppy seep he had found on his way south after leaving Easter.

The men drank sparingly, twisting their faces and swearing at the sharp taste of the water, but filling their canteens anyway. Last they brought the horses up, a few at a time, and watered them. The sun was setting, and Cloud called a halt. He figured they had gone far enough for one day. A little more of this and neither men nor horses would be much good in a fight.

They scattered out around the water to fix their suppers. Cloud ate silently, watching the men and listening to Quade Guffey give his appraisal of this country.

"It never will be worth two cents an acre," Quade declared to all who would listen to him. "Me, I like a place to have plenty of wood and water. You don't find no wood here hardly atall, and what little water you can get is so gyppy it'll go through you about as fast as you can drink it. No, sir, a hundred years from now there still won't be anybody livin' up here but Indians, and they just don't know no better."

Cloud walked over to where Seward Prince hunkered down with a coffee cup squeezed between his two hands.

"Prince," he said, "I was fixin' to have trouble this afternoon, till you spoke up. I'll tell you the truth—I never would've expected it from you. I'm much obliged."

Prince shrugged. "We've done come too far and put in too much misery to turn back whipped. I didn't see nobody comin' up with a better idee than yours. There's enough of us here to fix your plow if you didn't find the spring you was talkin' about."

A crooked grin crossed Cloud's bearded face. Sort of a left-handed support, this was. But it beat having no support at all.

Cloud and Miguel Soto rode in the lead, with outriders detailed on either side of the company. Men and horses had had a good rest, and Cloud held them to a steady jog trot. Such a gait could cover many miles in a day, yet not wear the mounts down. They had to protect the horses, for the horse was the common denominator. Whatever else a man might have was worth nothing to him in this big country without a horse.

Late in the morning Miguel Soto straightened and lifted his hand, pulling his horse to a sudden stop. He pointed ahead of him. Cloud squinted but saw nothing.

"It is down now behind a rise," Soto said. "Wait, maybeso it come back."

Cloud blinked. Heat waves were beginning to wriggle along the horizon line, looking almost like water. "Mirage, maybe," he said. "This country'll fool you that way sometimes."

Miguel shook his head. "No mirage. Maybe a horse, maybe a buffalo. But it is real. Look, there it is again!"

Cloud saw it this time. It moved toward them in a steady, deliberate pace. "Indian, I'll bet you. Better look sharp; there may be a lot more of them."

He had the captain's telescope in his saddlebag. He took it out and stepped down to rest it across his saddle.

"Rider, all right," he said finally. "Fact, it looks like two, ridin' double."

He lowered the glass and looked about for a depression, anything that might give the company some semblance of cover. He found nothing. The plain was unmarred by even so much as a buffalo wallow. He turned toward the men and made a circular motion with his hand. "Spread out in a circle and keep a sharp watch all around," he called. "Could be more than just the one of them."

The men deployed, and Cloud went back to the telescope. "What the . . ." He blinked and looked again. "It's a woman—a squaw. And she's got a child on the horse with her." He shook his head in wonder. "She can't help seein' us," he told Miguel, "but she's comin' right at us."

He kept watching, then he lowered the glass, his jaw dropping in astonishment. "It's *not* a squaw!" he exclaimed. "It's Easter!"

He telescoped the glass and dropped it back into the saddlebag, then swung up quickly onto the horse. "Hold your ground!" he yelled at the men, and spurred out to meet the woman.

Still wearing her buckskins, she dismounted as he

neared. She lifted the child down. Cloud jumped to the ground and grabbed Easter in his arms.

"Easter, Easter," he breathed, "I never thought I'd see you again."

He felt the tears on her cheek as she pressed hard against him, her hands strong upon his back. She didn't try to speak.

They pulled apart then, and Cloud looked down at the child. A white child—the Moseley girl!

Cloud dropped to one knee and put his hand under the girl's chin. "Joanna—that *is* your name, isn't it?"

The girl fearfully drew back from him. He realized that the long days' growth of beard and cover of dust made him look like some wild apparition to her. "I'm Cloud, honey," he spoke gently. "Don't you remember me?"

The little girl shook her head and put her arms around Easter's legs. Haunting fear dwelt deep in her wide blue eyes. The child's clothes were dirty and torn, but Cloud could see no sign that she had been harmed. "Easter," he spoke anxiously, looking up, "is she all right?"

"Scared to death but not hurt. She's seen a lot—been through a lot."

"That," Cloud said, "is a mortal fact." He stood up and gripped Easter's arms. "And you, Easter? How about you?"

She dropped her chin. "I'm all right." He saw grief in her eyes.

"What is it, Easter? Did you find your baby?"

She shook her head. "I was too late. It was dead."

He tightened his grip on her arm and said a quiet "Oh" in sympathy.

"It was always a sickly baby," she said. "I told you that. The women did what they could, but they couldn't save it. It was the white blood, they said."

He took her in his arms and held her again, wanting to

give her comfort but not knowing how. He expected her to cry, but she didn't. Likely she'd been through that and was finished with it.

He said, "It was our fault, I reckon—mine, for ever findin' you."

"No, Cloud, it's too late now to blame anyone. That wouldn't help. Likely it would've died anyway, even if I had been there. From the first, the women said it wasn't meant to live."

The little girl still held on to Easter's legs. Cloud looked down and asked, "How did you come to find her?"

"They brought her into camp last night. The women sent her to me because they knew I could talk to her." She paused, anxiety in her eyes. "Cloud, they're camped at the spring. I met the band on its way there soon after you and I parted. That's where the raiding parties were to come together."

Cloud nodded. "I had a hunch. That's why we were headin' thataway."

"But, Cloud, they know you're coming. They're waiting for you there."

Cloud looked off in the direction of the spring, his brow furrowed. "Bad luck. I'd hoped we'd shaken them off."

"You didn't. Spies came in last night to report. You've been watched all the way. Now they've prepared an ambush for you at the spring. That's why I slipped out in the night, to warn you. And to bring back this girl." She looked down with compassion, her hand resting lightly on Joanna Moseley's head. "One of the men took a liking to her, wanted to raise her as a daughter. That was why he saved her and brought her along. I think they probably killed the rest of her family."

Cloud nodded. "They did."

"I wanted to save this girl from going through the kind

of life I've had, Cloud. At her age, she'd be completely Indian in a year or two. She wouldn't remember anything else. Then someday, if she lived long enough, maybe white men would find her and take her away from the tribe, the way they did me."

She poured out her unhappiness in a thin, breaking voice. "Look at me," she cried. "I'm not a white woman, and I'm not an Indian. I'm a little of both, so now I'm not either one. I was happy enough as an Indian. Life was hard, but it was all I knew, so I thought nothing of it. Then you and the others took me away from that. You wanted me to be a white woman again. But I never was, really, because there was too much of the Indian in me. So I went back to the Indians.

"Those few days in camp at the spring have been enough to show me I'm ruined for that kind of life, too. I've learned too much of the white man's ways to be happy as an Indian again. They're two different worlds. I've got to live in one of them, but I'm not really fit for either one. How can anyone else decide what I'm supposed to be when I don't even know myself? Maybe you can tell me, Cloud; what am I?"

He gripped her hands and looked into her misty eyes. "You're a pretty woman, Easter, and I love you. I know *that,* and nothing else matters to me."

She leaned into his arms again, her head against his chest. "Sometimes I wish they'd killed me years ago instead of taking me with them. At least then I wouldn't have the awful choice to make."

He said solemnly, "It appears to me you've already made the choice. When you left that camp last night and came here with the girl, you burned the bridge behind you. You can't ever go back."

She nodded. "I know. It's finished now." She turned to look gravely behind her. "I wish I could take the best of that life and put it together with the best of the white man's ways. But you can't do that, can you? You can't mix them. You've got to go one way or the other, and burn the bridge!"

Cloud kissed her gently on the forehead. "I'm afraid it's that way. There may come a day when it's different, but not now. We've got to face things the way they are and do the best we can with them. I'll try to make you glad you came back, Easter."

For a moment she remained there in his arms, not saying anything. Then she pulled back. "Cloud, we've got to keep moving. Soon as they missed us this morning, they're bound to've known what I did."

"You figure they'll come after us?"

"I think they will. There are more of them than you know about, because there were men at the spring who didn't make the raid. They want your scalps, and they want your horses. They've got you up here a long way from home. Don't you think they'll try to get you?"

Cloud nodded. "I reckon. Was I *them,* I would." He turned her toward her horse. "We best be movin', then." He gave Easter a lift up onto her horse. He leaned down to the little girl. "Joanna, how's about you ridin' awhile with me? Miss Easter's bound to be tired."

Dubious, the little girl finally nodded. She watched Cloud closely, no longer fearing him but still not ready to accept him as completely human. He lifted her into the saddle, then swung himself up behind her, setting her in his lap. She turned her head to look up into his face. She said, "My daddy . . . we go see my daddy now?"

Suddenly Cloud felt his throat tighten. He looked across at Easter. "Doesn't she know?"

"What does a child her age know about death? How can you tell her?"

Cloud's eyes burned. Unconsciously he leaned down

and touched his cheek to the little girl's forehead. ''We'll take you home, Joanna.''

Once again he saw in his mind the big-shouldered old giant who had been the girl's father. He saw the quiet, determined mother, the brothers and sisters she'd never see again. He remembered most the girl Samantha, with the beautiful hair, the wistful eyes. He said again, whispering now, ''We'll take you home.''

Riding up to the company, he gave the men time to get over their amazement at the sight of Easter and the little girl. Briefly, he explained how Easter had slipped out of camp during the night, bringing Joanna with her.

''Boys,'' he said, ''this changes things. I know you all came to even some scores. We wanted to square up for Lige Moseley and his family. But the most important thing all along has been to get Lige's girl back. Now we've got her, and we can't afford to take a chance on losin' her again.

''Chances are the Comanches'll be comin' out to get us. Maybe we could whip them and maybe we couldn't. Now, I don't like to tuck my tail and run, but it looks to me like we got little choice now. We got the girl to think of, and Easter. I'll leave it up to you. If you want to stay and fight, we'll do that. If you want to dust it south, then we'll do that.''

He studied the faces of the men. Some of them looked grimly northward, their mouths set in a straight line that said fight. But then they looked at the pitifully ragged little girl, and compassion came into those dirty, bearded faces.

Seward Prince gave the reluctant answer for all of them. ''We'd best be a-savin' the girl.''

* * *

The sun was more than halfway down its western slant when the company once more reached the seep where it had spent the night. As the men rode in, dust lifted in front of them. Cloud spotted a small bunch of buffalo trotting away from the water in their lumbering, head-bobbing gait.

An idea struck him suddenly. "Miguel," he said to the Mexican a little in front of him, "hold up." He turned in the saddle. "Boys, before them buffalo get too far from the water, lope off yonder and shoot several of them."

The men spurred out. *Spa-a-a-n-n-g!* spat a rifle, and a buffalo pitched forward, kicking. More rifles roared. In a minute Cloud could see six or eight buffalo lying in the grass, either dead or jerking convulsively as life ebbed out of them in a flow of crimson. Men and horses and buffalo ran back and forth in confusion. Cloud shouted and lifted his hat, making a circle with it high above his head.

The men began moving back. Seward Prince rode in first, wiping sweat from his face onto his sleeve and leaving a streak of mud. He touched his rifle barrel, then jerked his head back from the blistering heat.

"What's the idee, Cloud? We need some fresh meat in camp, but not all that much."

Cloud said, "I got a purpose. Better go water out."

The men drank all they could stand of the gyppy water and filled their canteens. Then they let their horses in to take a fill. Hot and thirsty, the animals drank better than they otherwise would.

When everyone had finished, Cloud said, "Now let's take some ropes and drag them buffalo carcasses up into the waterhole. Way I figure it, time the Indians get here they'll be plenty dry. So'll their horses. But if we can foul the water, they won't be apt to drink it."

Prince looked northward, his eyes narrow. "Reckon that'll stop them?"

Cloud shook his head. ''I don't know. Maybe it won't, but it ought to help slow them down. It might make some of them turn back. And even if they catch up to us, an Indian on a give-out horse won't be near as troublesome. We'll have the edge, because our horses will have watered since theirs did.''

Quade Guffey said sorrowfully, ''In a country as short of water as this is, it sure does seem like a big waste to mess up a waterhole.''

Cloud shrugged. ''It'll clean up. But it'll be a long time.''

They had ridden until far into the night, then stopped for a dry camp without fires. At daylight they were up and preparing to ride.

Cloud was moving around, hurrying everybody up. ''Come on,'' he was saying, ''Let's get movin'. We got us a long lead, and we sure don't want to lose it.''

Miguel Soto appeared, his face grave. ''Maybeso we already lose it.'' He lifted his arm and pointed northward. Cloud turned and heard himself groan.

On a rise behind them he saw two men a-horseback, just sitting there watching them.

Indians!

Fourteen

QUADE GUFFEY SAW THEM AT ABOUT THE SAME TIME as Cloud did. He stood stiff-backed a moment, staring with his mouth open. He turned to Cloud and asked tightly, "Comanches?"

Cloud's mouth twisted as he watched. "They sure ain't none of *our* bunch!"

"But they *couldn't* have caught us already."

"You don't never want to figure on what an Indian can't do. They could've ridden all night. They knew what direction we were headed in. They could've eaten up the difference in the dark."

"Still, them two could just be a pair of strays that come up on us by accident."

Cloud asked, "You want to wait around and see?"

Quade shook his red head and lifted himself into the saddle, ready to ride. "No, thanks. If they got any business with me, I reckon they'll know where I'm at."

Sight of the Indians was all the group needed. As they rode away, Cloud looked behind him and saw a column of smoke spiral upward. In a moment it had turned into a grayish cloud, and he could see the dancing of flames licking through the dry grass.

Signal to the others, he thought. The main body of Indians must have sent scouts out to locate the white men as soon as it was light enough to see. Now the smoke, visible for miles around, would rally the scattered Comanches.

Looking at the spreading fire, Guffey commented sourly, "Damned prodigal with their grass."

Cloud said, "There's still a world of it left."

They rode steadily, moving part of the time in a jog trot, occasionally spurring up to an easy lope, being as merciful as they could on the horses but at the same time trying to gain on the pursuit. From time to time Cloud rode out to one side and turned to look back. Sometimes he saw Indians, sometimes he didn't. But one thing he knew: they were there, and they were coming as surely as sundown.

He looked apprehensively at Easter Rutledge and at the tiny girl who now sat in front of the doctor, Walt Johnson, in his saddle.

"Miguel," Cloud said, "there's no dodgin' it anymore; we're fixin' to have us a fight. The only thing we got a choice about is where to make our stand."

Miguel swung his hand in an arc. "It makes little difference. All this country, it is the same."

Cloud nodded, glancing back over his shoulder again. "Yeah, all wide open. But somewhere up yonder there ought to be somethin' to hide us a little—even a buffalo wallow if nothin' else."

Miguel humped his shoulders, showing he had little hope. "I do not know this country. I am only a scout. It is not for me to find something which is not there.''

They rode on, the smoke of the prairie fire hovering grimly behind them, a stark symbol of relentless pursuit. Cloud could see the growing tension in the faces of the men around him, in the blue eyes of Easter Rutledge. It was not so much the thought that they could not beat back the Indians. In almost any open battle anymore, the white man had the superiority in fire power. That was why the Comanche relied mostly on sneak attacks, on quick stabbing raids and immediate flight. But an Indian attack, even if repulsed, was almost certain to cause casualties out in the open this way. Worst of all, it was just as certain to result in a heavy loss of horses. Even victory in battle would be hollow indeed if many of the Texans were to find themselves left afoot out here in this waterless land, so many days from home.

The only one not showing the strain was little Joanna Moseley, slumped over a-doze in the lap of Walt Johnson. Cloud could feel his own nerves drawn tight. His mouth was dry, and he knew no amount of water could wet it.

He saw the old animal trails without realizing at first what they could mean, for he was too preoccupied with the Indians. Suddenly it came to him: Somewhere there was water, or had been water. The trails had been made by buffalo, drifting in to drink.

And where there was water, there was apt to be a depression of some sort—a hollow, a creekbed. Anything would serve better than this open country.

''Miguel,'' he said, ''we'll stop the company a little and let them catch a breath. You ride up this trail one way, and I'll go the other. We got to find out which direction the water is.''

He veered off to the left and let Miguel take the right. He rode possibly ten minutes. During that time he found two more trails converging into the one he was on. That was enough to satisfy him. He rode up onto a rise, fired his pistol into the air and waved his hat over his head. He saw the company pick up and move his way. On a far rise he saw Miguel Soto pause a moment, then come spurring. A moment after Miguel quit the rise, three horsemen appeared where he had been. Cloud saw smoke puff from a rifle.

He couldn't see Miguel, for the Mexican was behind the rolling hills. He saw part of the company split off and go back after the scout. For a moment the three Indians held their ground atop the hill and continued to fire. Now the sound of rifles began to reach Cloud, muffled by the distance. He never heard an answer he could attribute to Miguel. A premonition struck him. Without seeing, without hearing, he sensed somehow that they had brought down Miguel.

He could see the company sweep up the hill and drive the Indians down the far side. He looked in vain for Miguel's horse. The men turned back, dropping out of sight a minute or two as they came down from the rise. Later, for a few seconds, they came into view again much closer. They were riding fast. But Cloud had time to see they were supporting one man on his horse. Miguel!

Now the main body of the company came up to Cloud. He turned his horse around, leading the way up the trail in an easy lope. He slipped his saddle gun out of his scabbard and held it across his lap, on the ready.

He wondered how far it was to whatever he was looking for. The trail hadn't been used in a long time and was half grown over in grass. If it was a spring, it might have dried up. It *must* have, or there would be fresher sign of game. Even when he got there, it might not be any good for cover. It might be only an outcrop of rock or some such.

But in a time like this a man didn't stop to question.

He rode and hoped, and looked to his guns.

Off to the left he saw movement. Indians paralleling him and coming fast!

There *is* something up there, he realized suddenly. *They know it, and they're trying to beat us to it!*

"Come on," he shouted back over his shoulder. "Spur for all you're worth!"

It was a race, a hard race, the grass flying by beneath the driving hoofs of the horses. Cloud stood a little in the stirrups, leaning forward for better balance to give his horse a chance. He looked back again and again and found the company keeping up with him. Those who had gone to help Miguel were coming up behind, perhaps a quarter mile in the rear.

From Cloud's left came a paint-streaked Comanche warrior, desperately quirting a gray horse and heading straight for Cloud. The Indian swung up a short bow and with a quick flip of his wrist brought forward an arrow from the quiver at his back. Cloud saw the draw of the bowstring, saw the arrow streak toward him. He checked his horse, almost making it stumble. The arrow passed in front of him.

Can't waste a rifle shot, Cloud thought, *for God knows when I can load another*. He shifted the rifle to his left hand and used his right to draw his pistol. He fired once at the warrior and missed. The Indian had another arrow drawn back when Cloud fired the second time. The Indian's horse suddenly plunged forward, driving its nose into the ground. The Indian rolled and came up on his feet. By then some of the riders behind Cloud were in range. Half a dozen shots blazed, and the Comanche fell.

Ahead, Cloud saw what he had been looking for: scrub brush growing along the edge of a narrow dry wash.

No wonder they've tried to beat us to it, he thought. *Good place to make a stand.*

But the race wasn't won yet. The Indians paralleling him were still making a desperate run for it. Cloud turned to urge the Texans to ride faster. But he didn't have to. They'd seen the wash, and they'd seen the Indians. They were spurring, quirting, doing all they could. From here on it was going to be a test between horses.

For a few moments it was close. But gradually Cloud realized his company was going to win. The Indians' horses were playing out, falling back.

Tired out, Cloud knew—tired and dry. Fouling that waterhole had paid off.

Nearing the wash, Cloud reined to one side and stepped out of the saddle, dropping to one knee with his rifle ready. He waved the men on past, trying to get them into the protection of the wash. Some of them pulled up and jumped to the ground beside him, helping give cover for the others while they found a way to get the horses down the four-and-five-foot wall of the wash.

As the first wave of Indians came up—ten or twelve—rifles roared and black powder smoke billowed back into the Texans' faces. The Indians hauled up. A horse and a man fell. One wounded horse began to pitch, the Comanche rider trying to hold on. After several jumps the horse went to its knees, exhausted. In the interval when the Indians drew back uncertainly, Cloud and the others loaded their rifles and began to pull toward the wash afoot, leading their horses. Cloud walked backward, his eyes warily following the Indians.

He heard the pounding of hoofs to the left of him and glanced around to see the rest of his company coming up hard, bringing Miguel. From bellied-down Indians on a far rise, smoke puffed and bullets whined past the fast-moving riders. A horse went down rolling, its rider sprawling helplessly in the grass. Other riders pulled in, helping the dazed man up behind one of them. Cloud waved the newcomers into the wash.

Realizing the Rifles were about to make cover, the Indians began closing in. Cloud heard the whisper of spent arrows, shot from too far away to take effect. Those Indians who had rifles were using them, but the bullets kicked up little geysers of dust and clipped off cured grass, none doing any harm.

Spooked by rifle fire, some of the horses balked at picking their way down the steep sides of the wash. It took two men to get the horses down—one pulling from below, one pushing from above. Once a horse began to scramble and slide, the man beneath jumped back out of the way. Cloud heard a leg snap and knew they'd lost a horse. But they could do much worse if they didn't hurry.

Cloud was the last man into the wash. He dropped to his belly and rolled over the edge, tasting dirt. He held his rifle high in his right hand to keep it clean. He didn't have to give any orders. The men knew well enough what to do. They had scattered out along a hundred-foot width of the wash and peered over the edge, rifles ready. The flush of excitement rode high in their faces, but there was no panic. They'd loosed their horses in the center of the wash, some of the men stringing ropes to keep the animals from getting away.

They had set Miguel down on the ground. Cloud stepped to the Mexican's side and dropped to one knee, cradling his rifle across his left arm. Miguel had caught the wound high in the shoulder. Easter Rutledge knelt on the other side of the Mexican, trying with canteen and cloth to stanch the flow of blood.

Little Joanna Moseley pressed herself against the bank of the wash and screamed for her father, recoiling in terror every time a rifle blazed.

To Miguel, Cloud said, "Too bad, old friend."

Gritting his teeth, his face drained of color, Soto leaned his head back against the side of the wash. "Is all right, my frien' Cloud. I stomp a many snakes. Is sure thing, someday one of them bite me."

The little girl still screamed. Easter left Miguel to hold the wet rag tight against his own wound, and she moved to hold the little girl in her arms, to comfort her.

"Cloud," she asked anxiously, "what are our chances?"

"We got protection here, better cover than they have. All they can do is come in and try to run over us. Comanches hate to make a direct charge thisaway. They like the odds in their favor. That open country around us gives us the edge."

"There are more of them than of us," she pointed out.

"It ain't always *how many* that counts. Sometimes *where at* means a sight more."

She looked out over the edge. "A lot of them will be killed, I suppose."

He didn't answer, knowing it was pointless. She bit her lip. "I hoped it wouldn't be this way," she said. "I hoped they wouldn't catch us. They're still my people. . . ."

She looked down a moment. "Cloud, if it comes to that, I don't want them to take me back. I've betrayed them. I know better than anybody what they'll do."

A chill passed through him. "They won't take you, Easter."

The rifle fire quickened. Quade Guffey yelled, "Cloud, they're comin' at us!"

Cloud shifted the rifle back to his right hand and jumped to his feet. He saw forty or fifty Comanches angling toward them in a ragged line. The Indians were still three hundred yards away. The Texans held their fire until the horsemen were near enough for some accuracy. Then rifles began to blaze. Three horses fell, for horses were an easy target. Three men sprawled out on the ground. Two of them got up, one didn't. The Comanche line wavered and turned, sweeping off to the right without ever getting close enough for the Indians themselves to do any damage.

"Testin' us," Cloud said.

Guffey replied, "And I hope they found out what they was after. This ain't no bunch of helpless immigrants."

The Indians moved away from range of the Texans' guns and regrouped. Cloud stood back and wiped grimy sweat from his face and looked to the men. He made a quiet round of inspection and found they were all right.

Easter Rutledge had time now to bind Miguel's wound. Then she again held Joanna Moseley in her arms, gently patting the little girl's head. Joanna still sobbed a little, but no longer with the terror she had shown.

Now, thought Cloud dismally, *who's goin' to comfort Easter?*

The Indians came again, yelping and screaming even before they got in range. They presented an uneven front of painted horses and half-naked, painted men, feathers streaming. Even as he watched, his hands sweaty on the gun and his scalp prickling, Cloud could not escape the pagan beauty of it, the savage spectacle of these wild horsemen bearing down in a thunder of hoofs, a roll of dust.

Cloud took a look down his own line of waiting riflemen, saw the excitement flare in their eyes. He sensed the men were waiting for him to take the first shot. He picked a Comanche with a long headdress and leveled his rifle. It was going to be an easy shot, for the Indians were coming almost straight at them. It was so easy he almost hated to do it. He squeezed the trigger and flinched at the recoil. He saw the Indian slide off the horse.

Around Cloud the gunfire suddenly blazed, and more

Indians and horses went down. But the other Comanches kept coming.

Bound and determined! Goin' to get us or die tryin'!

Close by, Cloud heard a man gasp and turned to see Quade Guffey hunched over, gripping his left arm, cursing softly. Guffey cast a wide-eyed glance over the wash and began trying to reload his rifle. Blood ran down his arm, and he couldn't handle the rifle well enough to get another load in it.

Cloud shouted at Easter. "Easter, Quade's hit! Help him reload!"

Easter stood up and took the rifle. She fumbled with it, then the tears broke and she handed it back to Guffey.

"I can't . . ." she sobbed, sinking to her knees. "I can't. They're still my people."

Guffey, his teeth clamped tightly with his own pain, murmured, "It's all right, ma'am; it's all right." He drew his pistol and waited for the Indians to get close enough that he could use it.

Fire from the wash was gouging gaps into the Comanche line. The thunder of guns drummed into a man's brain until he could hear nothing except the guns themselves and the ringing sound they left driving in his ears. Cloud could still feel his hand sweaty on the rifle. He could taste dirt and sweat and could smell the warm odor of blood and the sharp biting tang of gunpowder that drifted around him in black clouds of smoke.

Now the Indians were close enough that he could see their painted faces, could see the mouths open in savage screams that barely penetrated his ringing ears. He could feel the vibration of the earth beneath the pounding hoofs. He fired the rifle and saw a man fall and knew he didn't have time to reload. He brought up his pistol and held it steady, waiting for a close shot.

He saw that the Indians were going to try to ride right

up over the wash and overwhelm the Rifles by sheer force of numbers.

Now it was short range—rifles empty and no time left to load them. It was pistols against Comanche short-bows. The Texans poured pistol fire into the screaming faces, the painted bodies that bore down upon them. The first of the line was right upon the wash now. The Indian horses slowed, trying to avoid a crashing fall into the gully ahead. The Comanches tried to whip them up, to keep them running. But the horses balked, and as they did, the Texans had time to cut down the Comanches with a blistering fire.

One horse fell, spilling his rider into the wash almost atop one of the Texans. The Texan whirled, grabbing his empty rifle and using the butt of it to brain the Indian before the man could move.

It was an insane swirl of dust and smoke, a bedlam of shouting, cursing men, of blazing guns and screaming horses. Around him Cloud could sense a frenzy of movement, but he forced himself to keep his gaze on what was just ahead of him, what was in range. He sensed that the Indian line had faltered, badly riddled.

He saw a magnificent warrior charging straight at him, a lance poised for the strike. Cloud's mouth was bone dry, his heart hammering. He wanted desperately to fire, but he had no idea how many shots were left in his pistol, if any at all. He couldn't fire until he knew he would not miss, for there might not be a second chance.

A few seconds seemed an eternity. He had time enough to study the Indian's painted face, red-streaked body, the buffalo shield with the scalp tied to it, the long blonde hair streaming out.

A cold fury welled up in Cloud. He felt the pistol buck in his hand, saw the Comanche jerk and come off the horse. The Indian hit the ground rolling and came over the edge of the wash, right on top of Cloud. Cloud shoved the pistol into the man's belly and pulled the trigger. There was only a dull click. He went down backward, the Indian's weight on top of him.

He could smell the grease, the woodsmoke odor that clung to the man, and he smelled the blood where he had caught the Indian in the shoulder. But there was strength in the man, even yet. The Indian grabbed at the knife on Cloud's belt and slipped it out of the buffalo-tail scabbard. Cloud gripped his wrist and wrestled with him for possession of the knife. He could feel the sweat breaking on his face, burning his eyes, and he knew the desperation in the Indian. But the Comanche was wounded, and this gave Cloud an edge. He wrested the knife from the man's hand and savagely slashed upward with it. The blade drove into the Indian's stomach. The man screamed and sagged forward. Cloud jerked the knife out and drove it forward again, plunging it hilt-deep between the warrior's ribs.

He pulled away then, letting the Indian slide to the ground. Cloud's eyes were afire from sweat and dirt, his hands desperately feeling over the ground for the fallen pistol. He found it and started to reload it. But even as he did so, he was aware that the gunfire was diminishing.

He blinked away the pain in his eyes and stood up. On the ground before the wash lay a pitiful scattering of dead and wounded horses, dead and wounded Indians. Off to the right, he could see the settling dust as the surviving Comanches retreated.

Quade Guffey stood beside him, holding his wounded arm, his sleeve crusting with blood and dirt, his face slowly paling from shock he had not had time to feel before.

"Reckon they've had a gutful, Cloud," he said thinly.

"They could take us, even yet. But they know it'd cost too much."

Already some of the men were climbing up out of the wash, searching for fallen Indians that might still be alive. Now and again they found one and finished him with a shot or the silent thrust of a knife.

Cloud knelt and picked up the buffalo shield where it had rolled into the wash. With trembling fingers he untied the scalp. No question to whom the long hair had belonged.

Seward Prince stepped up to Cloud and watched him finish the unpleasant job. He asked solemnly, "That girl back at Moseley's?"

Cloud nodded.

Prince cleared his throat and looked about uncomfortably. "Maybe she'll rest easy. We sure took that bloody vengeance the preacher was talkin' about." He nodded toward the scalp. "You want us to take that out yonder a ways and bury it?"

Cloud nodded. "It'd be the Christian thing, I suppose."

Prince said, "I'll get the preacher to go with me." He recoiled a little as the scalp passed into his hand. He paused before saying, "Cloud, you done all right. You sure done all right."

"Thanks, Prince," Cloud answered. "You all did." He turned toward Easter Rutledge, who sat in a huddle against the side of the wash, still holding the little girl. Easter didn't look up. She sobbed quietly, her shoulders heaving.

Regret passed through Cloud, and he wished they'd gotten away without all this slaughter.

Her people! And they always will be.

He put his hand on her shoulder and said gently, "It's all over now, Easter. We're goin' home."

*   *   *

The men had ridden wearily, drowsiness in their eyes. But as they came upon the first cabin of the Brush Hill settlement, they began to straighten. They broke their long silence and started talking. They waved at three small children and their mother who stood in the shade of a dog run. A little boy jumped on a horse and kicked him into a lope, moving out ahead of the rifle company to spread the news that the men were coming home.

By the time the men rode into the main part of the settlement, the people stood out beside the road waving, shouting them a welcome.

Cloud swung down as a couple of old men eagerly rushed to shake his hand.

"Glad to have you boys home again," one said with a grin.

"You kill aplenty of Indians?" the other pressed.

Cloud glanced back at Easter. "Enough of them, I reckon." Then, rushing to ask his own question before the two had time to throw another at him, he said, "I been worried about Captain Barcroft. Did he get in all right?"

One of the old-timers nodded. "Yep, couple of the boys brung him. He's over to the Lawton house."

Thanking them, Cloud remounted. He turned to Quade Guffey, who rode along with a stiff arm hanging at his side. "Quade, how's about you takin' the bunch on up to headquarters? I best stop in and visit with the captain first. See you directly."

Guffey nodded and gave a slight wave with his good hand. Cloud motioned for Easter to stay with him. He watched while the Rifles moved on down the dusty road, the settlement people walking out to shake hands with them as they passed.

A long way to Virginia, he thought, *a mighty long way. The war they're fightin' there don't seem to mean much here, don't even seem real somehow. We got our own war to fight, and we got the right men to fight it. Good men, every last one of them, the best men in the country.*

He pulled up in front of the Lawtons' stake fence. Hanna Lawton stepped to the door and saw them. She called back into the cabin, then came running. By the time Cloud had helped Easter down from her horse, Hanna was there, waiting to throw her arms about Easter. Cloud reached up and lifted the little girl down, setting her gently on the ground. They'd stopped at the creek a while back, and Easter had scrubbed the girl the best she could.

Hanna stood off at arm's length, looking Easter over. She said, "Cloud, we never expected to see her again. What . . . how . . . ?"

"It's a long story, Hanna," he said. "We'll tell you later. But first I better report to the captain. How is he?"

Cloud could see happiness in Hanna's smile. "He'll be all right, Cloud. It'll take a while, but he'll be all right."

Mother Lawton came out of the house, and Henry Lawton hurried along from the store. It took a few more minutes to get the howdies said to them. Then Cloud went into the cabin.

He blinked against the darkness and found Aaron Barcroft sitting up in a rocking chair, rocking impatiently, waiting for him. Cloud saluted. "Reportin' in, sir. We did what we went for."

As his eyes became accustomed to the room, he could see that the captain was pale and drawn. His eyes seemed drawn back into his head, but even so, Cloud could see the same spark which had always been there. The captain asked anxiously, "What about the little Moseley girl?"

Cloud smiled a little. "We found her, sir, and we brought her back. We found somebody else, too. We brought Easter Rutledge home."

The captain's eyes widened momentarily in surprise, then Cloud could tell the man was glad. Barcroft asked,

''She went after her baby. Did she find it?''

Cloud shook his head. ''It was dead, Captain.''

Barcroft dropped his chin, regret in his face. ''I did that to her,'' he breathed. He was silent a moment. Then, ''How about losses?''

''Two men killed, sir. Several shot up a little—none that won't get over it.'' He gave the captain a brief review of the campaign, stressing Easter Rutledge's part in it.

At last the captain said, ''I guess everybody needs to be laid flat on his back once in a while, just to force him to take time to do some thinking. I've done a lot of it the last few days. One thing I've realized is the wrong I did to Easter Rutledge. Now I'll never be able to right it.'' He frowned, his gaze on the floor. ''I suppose she still hates me. I don't guess she'll ever forgive me for what I did.''

''She'll forgive you, sir. You did what you thought was right. She respects that.''

The Lawtons came into the room, bringing Easter and the little girl. The captain stared at Joanna Moseley, and Cloud could see Barcroft's dark eyes melt into tenderness.

The captain whispered, ''Come here, little girl.''

Unsure of herself, the girl went to him. The captain reached out hesitantly and touched her hand and said in a tight voice, ''What's your name?''

So quietly the others could hardly hear, the girl said, ''Joanna.''

''How old are you, Joanna?''

With some deep thought, the girl held up three fingers.

''Three,'' the captain said. ''You know, I had a little girl like you once. Last time I saw her, *she* was just about three. You look like her—a whole lot like her.''

Innocently the girl asked, ''Where is she now?''

''She's gone . . . far away.'' The captain paused a long

moment, then said, "How'd you like to climb up here in my lap, Joanna?"

Hanna Lawton stepped forward to stop it, worry in her eyes. "Aaron, your wound!"

The captain waved her away. "It'll be all right," he said. Cloud lifted the girl into the captain's lap. The captain put his good hand on Joanna's shoulder and pulled her against his chest. He said to her, "I've been looking for another little girl to come and live with me, a little girl like the one I had. Would you like to be my little girl?"

Joanna murmured wearily, "It'd be all right, I guess."

The captain began to rock the chair gently while he held Joanna. Presently the girl looked up and said, "You're crying! What're you crying for? Did somebody hurt you?"

The captain shook his head and drew the girl closer. "No, child, nobody hurt me." He kept on rocking, and Cloud turned away.

On the porch outside, Easter said, "I thought I'd hate him as long as I lived, but I don't. I can't hate him anymore. I can only feel sorry for him."

Hanna Lawton said, "He's a good man, Easter. He's hard to understand sometimes, but he's a good man." She held silent a moment, then smiled uncertainly. "Easter . . . Cloud . . . he's asked me to marry him."

Surprised, Cloud blurted, "Well, I'll be damned!"

Hanna said, "It's a cruel thing, but I'm almost glad he was wounded. It forced him to lie still a long time and think. And it gave me a chance to be with him."

Cloud told her, "He's a smart man, Hanna. He wouldn't have overlooked you forever."

"Maybe he would and maybe he wouldn't. It doesn't matter now. He's asked me, and I told him yes."

Cloud said, "Looks like you'll have to be a mother to

the little Moseley girl. I hope you won't mind that."

Hanna shook her head. "She'll help. Didn't you see his eyes while ago? For a few minutes there he was happy—happy like he hasn't been in years. His daughter was one loss *I* never could've made up to him. But maybe this little girl can." Hanna turned then to Easter. "Your clothes are still hanging where you left them. You'll have a home here just as long as you want it."

Cloud took Easter's hand. "Easter's goin' to have a home of her own, Hanna."

Fondly watching the couple, Hanna said, "I'm glad."

When they were alone, Cloud led Easter down to the creek. They stood together beneath the trees, listening to the soft rustle of the leaves, the quiet murmur of the water. Easter looked northwestward toward the land she had left, the home to which she could never return.

Cloud said gently, "You've given up a lot, Easter, and there's some of it I know can never be made up to you. But maybe in time I could help you forget. Maybe I could make you happy."

She leaned to him, her head against his shoulder. Her arms went around him, and she said in a soft voice:

"You will, Cloud. You will."